THE DOT

Tim

Matchstick Literary
1-888-306-8885
orders@matchliterary.com

Prologue

There was a dot. This dot did nothing extraordinary and had nothing but have a boring existence until the dot withered and disappeared. Here and there, the dot heard news of lucky people who experienced trials far greater than its own day-to-day life routines. *No,* the dot thought. This the dot could not have, then from nowhere and seemingly for no reason the dot was given a power to change this. Something that was absolute and trumped all else.

The dot was about to begin but something happened to agitate it. "No, no, no, no.", "Please don't let yourself go.", "Don't forget what you came here to do." it tried to tell itself, but it knew at the back of its mind that it was already overwhelmed by it. It would happen, from out of nowhere and it would lose sight of it all. With just his will, the omniverse was destroyed then created again even bigger, but then willed it out of existence and brought everything back to what it was.

It stared in wonderment. *This power,* he thought, *with no upper limit, something that surpasses all. If It wills it to be done then it is so.*

"Just don't become lost." it said. But even it didn't listen to its own words. And as pitiful and honestly comical as it was, it happened just like that.

Stage 0

BOY

The boy whimpered as the man struck at his face again. The little boy's blood splattered on the wall. The boy held his face in his hands, shielding himself from any more strikes to his face, but also hiding tears. The man beating him yanks the boy's hands away from his face shouting, "Stop being a little bitch, boy! This shit is fucking embarrassing!"

"Lift up the box again." the man ordered.

The boy struggled to get up, shaking with his face full of tears. The boy was moving slowly, far too slowly for the man's patience. The man grabbed the boy by his shirt and threw him against the box.

"Do you see the box?" the man asked.

"Yes." said the boy.

"Then lift it up!" the man yelled.

The boy lifted the box but only so slightly before he gave out and involuntarily dropped the box. The man grabbed the boy by the head and said, "Now tell me what happened."

"I dropped the box." the boy answered.

The man took the boy's head and smashed it against the box. The boy fell down but caught himself.

"Headbutt the box." the man said.

The boy headbutted the box, but not to the satisfaction of the man. He took the boy's head and smashed it against the box again. Now making a huge bloodstain in the side of the box.

"Best do it harder, boy." the man suggested.

The boy did it harder, as hard as he could and it hurt so badly. This however was still not enough for the man. He took the boy's head and kept slamming it against the box until his arm grew tired.

The boy had not yet blacked out but was clearly not all there either. He could feel himself almost passing out.

"You've said you've gotten stronger, right?" the man asked.

"Yes." the boy responded.

"Then, what is this I'm seeing here? You're still weak. You can't even lift a fucking box. You've just stayed the same. A little weak punk ass kid." the man said, looking disappointed. "You know what happens to the weaker ones, don't you?"

"The…" the boy could barely speak but he continued. "The stronger ones have their way with the weaker ones." the boy finally let out.

The man unzipped his pants and put the bloodied, beaten boy to the ground. The boy, like always, was at the mercy of the man, he would put objects inside of him, beat him all while roughing him up from behind. After the man was finished having his way with the boy, he threw him to the ground and dropped the box on top of him. Making him unable to move, while crushing his frail body.

The boy stared up at the ceiling, unable to move, this feeling of being helpless burned at him. He tried to move but fainted instead from exhaustion. The boy woke up to find the box was still on him. He struggled again and again until he was finally out from under the box. The boy was relieved and feeling victorious, awoke once more to find that it was only a dream. This drove the boy to tears, he covered his face to begin wailing. Then a certain force was felt on the box. The boy looked and saw the man again.

The man stood with one foot on the box. The man lifted the box with ease and lifted the boy up and held him against the wall.

"Look at yourself, anyone else can do this, anyone except you."

He threw the box at him. Then slapped him repeatedly across the face until his hand went numb and was dripping with blood. "You're completely at the mercy of everything around you."

The man dragged him through the house and down to the basement, where it was very cold. The man then locked the door and that was the last sound the boy heard for the longest time.

The boy was shocked to the core. Being down there before, he already knew everything around him. But just as before, it still scared him just as much as the first time he was here. He would sit there in the middle of the room, waiting for the next time the door unlocked. Not knowing what would happen next, not knowing if he would be up to the next task.

The boy now sat alone in the cold dark room that was the basement of the house. He was thinking, lost in his thoughts, thinking critically and intensively of his own insignificance. The boy has failed at everything brought to him and could not perform the slightest action to complete any of the given tasks. He had nothing to offer, with nothing to show but his scarred and molested body with a beaten face. The only act he was capable of doing was to sit there, shivering uncontrollably.

"A complete waste." the boy said. *I'm a complete waste,* the boy thought. The man said one thing before pushing the boy back to his basement home.

"Why do you exist? Why did you have to be a reality? Someone else could have been here, anyone but you."

That shook the boy, like an echo in his head that wouldn't go away, "If I were to go, maybe that would suffice for someone who could do much better than me."

If I would off myself right now, no one would be hurt by it and the man would even be relieved. I just don't want the burden I bring to anyone else. the boy thought. The boy hurt himself plenty for this and over time did end up enjoying it, in a way of course.

It became his hobby, however; he did attempt suicide several times but something always held him back. Maybe it was fear; some of it, that was for certain. But something was different, hard to explain really; the feeling of total defeat. Although this feeling was all that the boy felt but maybe it won't be an absolute defeat as long as the boy put up some effort, at the very least.

However, this time would prove to be different as he knew of a wooden bar that was perpendicular from the pole near the stairs where a light was supposed to be lit, that could support his weight. It was definitely high enough to where his feet wouldn't touch the ground. He wasn't sure if it would hold his weight as there was a leak from the ceiling that dampened and thus weakening the already frail looking bar.

But at this point, he had already exhausted all the other options, so he had to try. He tied a noose or at least tried to. It took him some time before he came up with a rough looking one that could get the job done. Using the stairs as a point to drop from, he made sure everything was right.

As he leapt forward and closed his eyes, the wood immediately snapped at his weight and he fell to the ground. He would have succeeded if the weak moist wood held up instead of breaking. He could've been gone, but his desire was abruptly stopped.

At least that is what the boy wished had happened. The wood was not weak. In fact it was surprisingly firm, holding the rope and the boy's weight with ease. He choked as he dangled.

It hurts, it all hurts so much.

He wished for some sign even at the last second that made everything he thought untrue. Yet, there was nothing but his vision fading to black. The loud creaking sound of the wood made by the swaying of the rope, becoming ever more distant.

However, in another person's ears, the sound was awfully loud. A woman who was paid to service the man grew uncomfortable by the sound, while the man also grew annoyed by it.

"Wait here." the man said as he went down into the basement.

The woman was curious about what exactly was going on. Filled with paranoia, she picked up her purse and followed the man. The man went to the basement and saw the little boy, emaciated and choking with tears in his eyes, the man laughed.

The woman came down and felt the cold that made her shudder. She hardly saw anything but pitch black at first, but as her eyes adjusted, she could make out the man and someone else. She lit her lighter and the sight she saw was so horrid to her.

The man yelled and rushed towards her shouting, "I told you not to come!"

Instinctively, she pulled out her pistol and fired off. The man dropped and the woman froze in place. The sound of the fire spooked the boy and he opened his eyes regaining some sight.

Upon the scene of the dead man he could only stare, she fired and shot him. She took the man down, not him. Upon his flailing, now trying to stay conscious he caught the woman's attention. The woman held the boy while burning the rope, then helped the boy down yet the boy still fainted, although still breathing. She lifted the boy up and carried him out. Surely the scene would lead directly to her, and the boy would surely give her away. The look in his eyes gave her that answer for certain, or maybe her paranoia was getting to her.

As the boy drifted in and out of consciousness, he found himself reliving past memories of his time in the cold basement. There were drawings of little people on a giant sheet of paper staring back at him. He continued to draw on every sheet of paper there was until every part of the basement wall was covered in his drawing. These drawings are what became his friends that would never leave him.

The boy would get into quite some conversations with them and he greatly enjoyed their company. It was amazing how well the boy related to them, it was as if they were an extension of himself. The boy never really thought of himself being lonely anymore. Whenever he felt lonely though, with the "me" time he had, he wouldn't be far away from them at all. He was comforted by them as he slept. When he was thrown back in by the man into the basement, he knew, they were always there.

Eventually and all too suddenly things started to change, the relationship between the boy and the pictures seemed to have been altered. Now, every time the boy went to sleep he would see them staring at him. He closed his eyes shut, too afraid to open them again. Even when he was awake, he would fake being asleep for hours before he had the courage to open his eyes.

Every morning was a battle just to do just that. When the man was finished with the boy, he would throw him to the basement where the pictures would stare back at him menacingly. He expected them to harm him the same way the man did. The boy could only stare back in cold fear. He would swear that one of the drawings moved once, then again and again it would happen as if it was happening right in front of the boy's eyes.

They would start to say things to the boy of how they would harm him as he slept. How they would do unto him as the man did. The boy wouldn't sleep for days, but eventually one does succumb to sleep and they get it whether they want to or not. The boy would fall asleep and the drawings would come towards him, only the boy could still see them as they horribly brutalized him.

They took a pole and shoved it up his anus, shoving it in as deep as they could. Stretching and tearing the rest of the boy's body. Next they pulled off all of his appendages, doing it as slowly as possible, he could hear the sounds of the bone cracking and popping. It carried on endlessly like an echo in the basement. The flesh tore, exposing the warm blood slowly oozing out and when the arteries ruptured, blood squirts from the boy's body. They then wrapped and dragged him in chains around the basement, but the boy could only scream. He screamed as loudly as his lungs would let him. He kept screaming until his voice went out, even until he gurgled as blood filled his lungs.

He let them do as they wished. He was in too much fear to resist, to fight back, to do anything. He screamed until he woke up just to see them again, too afraid to even scream, too afraid to touch the picture to take them down, too afraid to do anything, but sit there to shiver and cry.

He now constantly stared at the ground to avoid their gaze, their judging eyes with evil intent. When it was dark, he could notice only their eyes staring him down, studying waiting for the next opportunity they would get. The boy grew some courage and grabbed some black coloring material and still with his eyes facing the ground, he followed his peripheral vision.

The boy shakenly walked toward the wall and crossed their eyes out. He then went back to the middle of the room and sat down. Even though he couldn't see their eyes anymore, he could still feel them looking at him somewhere in the dark.

The boy stared at the drawings he made and noticed that as the morning approached, he could now see the mistake he made. The drawings with their eyes crossed out seemed to now furiously stare at the boy, only adding more emphasis to their eyes.

Really, he just couldn't escape this nightmare that was his hell. This hell that was his reality, and he just made it worse for himself. Everything he tried to do only signified one thing: he was a complete waste.

"A complete waste", the boy said. *I'm a complete waste* the boy thought.

The man said a certain statement to the boy before throwing the boy back into the cold, dark basement home.

"Think of all the kids, all the people with such great potential who could've done great things, accomplished so many great feats unimaginable, done good to mankind itself and you just keep existing here. You're a waste of space. That's a pitiful joke, so pitiful it's not even funny, a 'fuck you' to everyone else that's worth something but you. That's what you are, that's your entire life."

Everyone else is worth something, the boy thought. *Everyone else is worth something*, his mind echoed again.

"And I'm worth nothing." the boy finally said.

What the man said had slain the boy down. The statement punctured his mind, 'a waste of space', butchered it from the surface in, a 'fuck you' to everyone else, 'everyone else is worth something' and killed it.

The boy grew to hate his own existence as well. He felt as if he should be punished and he did punish himself, in a way it was a release out of his self-loathing. He would head butt the steps on the stairwell until he passed out and when he awoke, he would do it again. This left him with a bloody face with parts of his face smashed in and broken, and the steps were wet with blood and warm moist flesh.

He was ridiculous with himself; he would run into poles until tears fell and his knees buckled or couldn't stand, at times he would black out from the trauma or pass out from mere exhaustion.

When that wasn't happening, he would spend the rest of his time crying. He thought of himself as pathetic, since he would try to stand and move but his body wouldn't budge as if it is too tired to do so, it seems to put all its effort into crying instead.

The boy did dream however, it was only a dream but he still thought of it immensely; of the ideal man he fantasized himself to be, or to become. He went to the far back part of the basement, which was extremely low and cramped and by the time you reached the back you had to crawl.

There he drew the man as tall as his small fragile body would allow and as big and wide as he could get on the low end of the ceiling. The ceiling was really easy to reach as the far back portion of the basement floor was touching the ceiling.

This man stood taller than the rest, he was bigger than the rest, and now that the picture was finished, it gave the basement a different perspective. It was as if the way the picture was drawn, made all the people with crossed out eyes look extremely frightened.

He was the strongest, the boy thought. He looked around and saw the people once more.

They are in awe yet scared of his wrath, he thought again.

The boy had even given himself a picture. One of them was this ideal man standing before a pile of meat and water. The meat were people who stood in his way and the water were their tears.

On the back of the paper there were a group of people surrounding him and below, nobody was there because in an instant he made sure that there was nothing left of those that had challenged him.

On the road the woman drove wildly, her hands sweating as they held and shook the steering wheel. *Finally,* she thought with the little peace of mind that she had. She stopped the car in front of a house at the end of the block.

The woman parked her car in the driveway and stared at the young boy's disfigured face, dried tears from his eyes, drool from his mouth and the horrible bruises that covered his neck; this was from the rope he used to hang himself. Not only that but the boy was extremely bloody, cuts and gashes lined his face and parts of his head were caved in, parts of exposed bone, other parts actually looked fractured.

The boy's clothes were completely soaked in blood, no telling if under those clothes was there anything similar to his face. No doubt that this boy was a horrid sight to see. Her mind raced as she tried to make a plan out of this mess she found herself in.

The man watching over this business wouldn't take too kindly to some boy in his house and definitely wouldn't take the story of everything that transpired and how things just went down tonight, she thought.

Even though the house was very huge, the head wouldn't be so keen on letting a total stranger in the house, especially one that wasn't one of his employees, she thought with disgust. The boy was sound asleep so he wouldn't awake anytime soon, at least that's what the woman had told herself.

The woman took the blankets she kept in the back seat and covered the boy. Once she was done, she exited the vehicle. She then went to the door and knocked. She didn't have keys, only the head did, and he would give out the time each day he would be in. She looked at her watch.

He should be in by this time, she thought. She hesitantly knocked again.

But the door opened before her knuckle even reached the door. It was one of the head's delegates, and he wasn't happy at the sight of her. He grabbed her by the neck and pulled her inside.

"You weren't supposed to be back by now! So tell me just what the fuck happened?!" he demanded.

"H-he w-wasn't in the mood. I guess his wife had called so he decided to back out." she said nervously, choking out her words

"You know the head isn't going to like this, once I tell him." he said.

"You can tell him so much, to the point that you can give me an hour to myself." she said.

"And why in the flying fuck, would I do that?" he said, demanding an answer.

"I have some extra money I left in the car, if you would I could go back and get it for you." she answered, bribing the man.

"Alright, then. Get moving and do whatever you got going. I'll leave you alone for an hour." he said.

She went back outside to the back of her car and saw the boy again. The wound around his neck had swelled up tremendously. The blood made the boy's clothes and the blankets that covered him very sticky. As she picked him up, she felt parts of his stomach and back; it was confirmed that the rest of his body resembled his face if not worse.

As she picked him up she felt him breathe heavily, she couldn't say if it was from the pain caused by her touching his wounds or what, but she was at ease hearing him breathe. She wrapped the boy up in the blankets and paused. She did not notice how small and incredibly light he was until now, she had to be very gentle with him.

"Alright." she said concealing the boy's face then she entered the house.

The man was still standing there waiting expecting her to deliver on the deal. She did give him five hundred dollars and he grinned slightly.

"That there, those blankets, I suppose that's what you need an hour for." he asked rhetorically. The woman said nothing in return.

"Whatever, you got an hour before I tell him anything." he said.

Still silent, she ran upstairs. She looked around frantically and soon as sense came to her, she wanted to throw herself off a bridge for being so stupid. The only place she could hide him was in her closet. The woman unwrapped him in her closet and she could actually see how small he was when compared to a shoe box in her closet.

He was extremely emaciated, his body looked like it was just skin and bones.

"The poor boy, my poor boy." she said.

She began to get lost in her thoughts. Eventually, she snapped out of it and washed the blood from the towels and cleaned the boy with it afterwards. The boy was then finally clean of the blood. She was amazed by herself as she washed towels again and threw them in the basket. The boy had been bleeding relentlessly when she found him, but she couldn't trust the hospital that was miles off. Trusting the cops would've been a mistake,too. This was her only option, at least she convinced herself enough it was that.

As soon as she closed the closet door, she realized that an hour had already passed. She went to the bed, sat on the edge and waited. *It looked like Zefron held true to his promise this time*, she thought. There was movement in the closet made by the boy; he was waking up. The woman heard the movement too and was about to move to the closet until she heard the doorknob rattle.

The door opened and the head stepped in, he smiled at her. "So Zef told me your night was unsatisfactory, yeah." he said. "Nothing in return and no money."

"Well, Amy you have to give me something. You just can't come back empty-handed."

He yanked her by her hair and she let out a small scream, wincing in pain. The boy now fully aware of himself, peeked out from the closet door to see that it was the woman who killed the man in the basement and now she was at the mercy of another.

It grieved the boy to look at her. Something he couldn't, something he would never do, she had done it. The man yanked her hair again and slapped her. She put her hands up covering her face as she looked at the ground, her tears starting to form.

"Look at me." the man said.

She looked at him and he slapped her again. She covered her face and whimpered.

This looked all too familiar to the boy. It was all too painfully familiar to him and it was all too soon.

The man unzipped his pants and forced the woman's face towards his penis and forced her mouth to open. He held her head and went back and forth, in a jerking motion. And then shoved her head down on it, forcing her into taking everything in. Soon she started struggling, but the man held her in place, forcing her to stay. Her eyes became teary and her mouth sounded obstructed trying to get air.

"Fuck yeah, sweetheart." the man said.

The man finally let her go and she desperately gasped for air. He then slammed her on the edge of the bed before she could catch her breath. He forced her to bend over, forced her head in the covers and penetrated her.

The boy decided to step out but the woman glanced at the closet and their eyes met. The woman motioned her head "No" andthe boy stepped back inside.

"Now, who do you belong to?" the man said.

"The head." she mumbled.

He hit her at the back of the head. "Why don't you say it clearly, bitch meat?" he demanded.

"I belong to the head." she said loudly.

He finished, slamming her face down into the covers and slapping her rear.

"Have a nice night, sweetheart." he said as he walked out, closing the door.

She heard the door close as she still laid there. She eventually lifted her head to see the little boy, who was still hesitant to step out. She eventually stumbled over to the closet to see him. The boy's face was still horrid to look at, all the dents, cuts and bruises but through all of that still came those curious eyes that looked scared at the same time.

She smiled so warmly at the boy. Now that she was closer to him, she could see that he was shaking. Slowly, she grabbed for the boy and as she tried, he backed away defensively. She held out her hand and waited for the boy to claim it. But he just stood there staring at her in fear. She opened something for him, a snack to give the boy; a brownie. She placed it in the closet along with other blankets.

"Sleep nicely," she said.

She cleaned herself and went right to bed, she could see him staring at her as she slept. After viciously eating the brownie, the boy could only do what he had grown used to doing and thought of how the woman's treatment closely resembled his own, and how she accomplished something that seemed only fantasy in the boy's mind. These hard burning thoughts stalked the boy into his sleep.

The man was roughing the boy from behind, as he pleasured himself at the boy's expense, he told the boy to say what he was.

"Weak meat." the boy said.

"You can do anything you want to me." the boy said as what was rehearsed.

He bit the boy's ear saying "You're damn right."

He then twisted the boy's head towards him and started biting it, damaging the boy's neck. Once he was done he tossed the boy into the basement, saying one word before closing the door, "Fuckboy."

At the bottom of the stairs, it held the boy's flesh and the blood from the self-mutilation he acted upon. The man couldn't see it as it was dark for him to notice but as the boy's eyes adjusted he could see it clearly even in his fragile state.

The ideal man he fantasized covered his vision, the people on the walls around him were frozen in fear of the I. It's weird that the ceiling closes in on the floor at the far end of the basement. With the way it was structured and the way the paintings were set up, it looked like a hall.

The I was coming down the hall with frightened bystanders watching in horror. I, the boy thought, the ideal man the boy hungered ferociously to become. The I stayed with the boy locked in his mind never to go away.

Amy tossed and turned in her bed, her mind refusing to sleep again. She slept three times in one night and awoken three times that same night, from the same nightmare she dreamed three times in a row. Only it wasn't just a dream but a painful memory that drove her to tears every time she was forced to relive it.

Everyone held her down while she looked down at her pregnant belly. They were forcing an abortion while she was awake. The dead small limp body was pulled out from her and the bloody mess they had left her in while she screamed for her baby that was already gone. This etched a deep emotional scar, a void now that she hoped to fill.

She didn't sleep the whole night. Once sunrise broke she instinctively went to the closet only to see that the brownie she had placed was gone, but the blankets were unused. *It's a start,* she thought as she laid her eyes at the sleeping boy. Her shift would not start until nighttime. She closed the door and rested during the day. The boy however, started to move. He peered out of the closet to see the woman still asleep. *Her name,* the boy thought.

He remembered last night when she smiled at him. *So warm and welcoming* he thought. He also saw the bruises, that swollen part of her face and that part that had dripped blood. He saw her sleeping peacefully for the moment.

The boy sat there staring at the woman with such intrigue. She was awake now and every time she would go and check the closet, the boy would act as if he was asleep. She would stare at him and put her hand out to caress him, but the boy on instinct would involuntarily flinch before she could touch him. She knew he wasn't asleep; in part of his persistence, his sudden flinching gave it away.

Whenever she could, she would save her own food and give it to the boy. The portions were so small that sometimes she couldn't eat any of it and gave it all to the boy, keeping him full instead. She however, would starve. She saw that the night was approaching as she glanced outside.

She had spent the whole day in her room knowing that the boy was staring at everything she did. She did get what she could from the kitchen. She cut her clothes and sewn them together into smaller ones. She continued to periodically check on him just to make sure he was well. Though it was very excessive, it would ease her mind for the time being.

She went and checked her watch. *Just a little while longer,* Amy thought. She opened the closet door and saw him this time not pretending to be asleep. Giving him one last gaze, she thought of something and realized what was he to do in this closet besides stare a hole through her. She thought hard about this as she left.

Just off her shift, she was very successful. She had given most of the money to the delegates and kept some to herself as she brought a few things for him and went upstairs. Crayons and paper for the boy. She laid it down in front of him and closed the door knowing of course that the boy wouldn't touch it while she was looking at him. She knew that she had to give him some space. When she wasn't doing something for the boy, she would be constantly reminded of that night and her lifeless baby.

The boy she saw was a blessing but in reality, what it was really, it is just another child that brought back terrible memories. She however did not try to think of this in the slightest. She tried hard busying herself with other tasks like cleaning her room so she wouldn't think of it as she fell asleep.

The boy now with crayons and paper, drew this large and powerful man, an all-powerful being capable of anything that he wanted. He would draw how this man would destroy others with his bare hands. Describing his pure strength, how it was unlike any other. How he was the only true champion. How no one would even consider to challenge this unstoppable and indomitable force.

This was something that began to take over the boy's mind both awake and asleep. As he was disturbed by the sound of muffled screams, he peered at Amy from out of the closet. She was in tears sitting at the edge of the bed, the boy decided to step out of the closet. Amy turned around by the sound of the closet door creaking. She saw the boy staring right back at her in tears.

She placed her hand on her belly still staring at him. The boy was in terrible conflict with himself. He couldn't seem to place the woman. She reminded him so much of himself that it seemed that they were the same, but then again not at all same. She actually got the job done, where he failed and ultimately gave up.

Hanging from that wood, he gave up on everything, his dream and his hope. This woman didn't do that. *Then maybe,* the boy thought harder. It was possible all along and he just couldn't see it, or maybe he just wasn't as strong as she was. The boy's anger grew towards himself, and he loathed himself immensely for the moment when he decided to end himself in the basement.

Maybe this was the sign the boy was looking for back in the basement, a time for retribution. But as soon as the boy tried to see it differently, a voice with a fierce tone of hostility had taken its place.

"That's not what this is at all about, boy. This is all a joke that can actually be laughed at. Your life is a waste, and you can't change that. Together with the countless times for retribution in that cold basement." the voice sounding as if it's mocking him.

"Now, this is the world saying 'fuck you' to you, as you did by just staying alive, a joke that's actually worth laughing at." the voice said.

The boy disregarded the voice and tried to force it in the back of his mind.

No this woman isn't here for punishment. No, the boy thought, *this woman is helping me.*

"What a sorry case, being in denial and lying just to stop you from killing yourself again." the voice said before receding back into his mind.

The woman stretched her arms out, her face looked like she was begging the boy to embrace her. The boy stepped back and more tears from Amy came rolling down her cheeks. Seeing her tears, the boy hesitated and readjusted himself. He was contemplating what to do. She had been nothing but lovely so far but he was still hesitant about it. He looked at her face and saw what she'd done; she's helping him.

He was still hesitant, still frightened, but still he continued moving. Amy's face changed as if she couldn't believe herself. He was coming towards her, but he was moving slowly as if ready to turn away to run at any second.

"That's it come on, I just want to love you." she said, encouraging and beckoning him towards her..

Eventually he was right in front of her, she pulled him closely to her chest and hugged him fiercely. Amy seemed to tighten her grip on him every second, she could be like this with her boy forever. She carried him around and sat on the bed with her still holding him.

The boy was shaking but eventually relaxed and soon slept. When he woke up the next morning, Amy's arms were still around him. He looked at her; he saw that she had fallen asleep but still got ahold of him. He tried to move but was unable to get out of her arms. The movement woke Amy. She soon stood up and walked around the room still carrying him. The boy felt slightly uncomfortable as she went about the room still holding him. Amy still hasn't left the room and it's almost noon.

"Hungry." the boy said.

"W-wha?" Amy said as if slipping back into reality. "Oh yes, of course." she said, regaining herself.

She picked him up and had him sit in his closet to eat while she tended to laundry, cleaned the room. The boy on the other hand finished his lunch. She looked at him in the closet and saw some of his drawings.

"Oh, what's that?" she said as she was reaching for one.

The boy snatched the drawings away to keep them to himself. He eyed her unsurely.

"It's fine." she said. "You like to keep things to yourself. I can easily respect that."

She stared at him for some time and said. "My name is Amy, what's yours,?"

The boy shook his head and told her that he had no name.

"Then that means I can give you one." she said, excitedly.

"No." the boy said in defiance. "I will, when I'm ready."

She rubbed his face, he jumped slightly at the touch of her palm. "As you say." she responded.

She checked her phone and saw a warning from Katlyn, a friend of hers. The next few moments weren't going to be pleasant.

"I'll be back shortly." she said.

She closed the closet door and turned to sit on her bed. A few minutes later the door opened.

"What in the fuck is this?" a man said.

He held up a newspaper, flashing it to her face. "'A Man found dead after a gunshot was heard'." he read out of the newspaper.

"What does that have to do with me?" Amy asked.

He hit her with a strong backhand. Wincing in pain, she covered up her face with one hand trying to prevent herself from receiving another hit.

"The fuck do you mean?! This is the same house you went to the other night! The goddamn gunshot was heard around the same time you were there!" he yelled furiously.

"I knew nothing about any gunshot." she said nervously.

"Give me that fucking purse!" he yelled. He didn't even let her give it to him, he took it and pulled out a pistol.

"So, what the fuck is this?!" he exploded. Rage now evident in his face.

She hesitated and said "It was for pro-".

Before she couldn't even finish her sentence. The man slammed her against the wall. He punched her in the face, each time harder than he last. She started sinking down to the floor but the man held her up and punched her in the gut really hard. Blood started shooting from her mouth.

She was crying in tears saying it was a mistake, begging him to stop.

"Hey call the head in here quick!" he shouted out of the room.

More men rushed in and beat her down. They then held her up, the boy was about to step out, but at the sight of him she screamed "NO!!!!"

He stepped back frightened. They continued to hoist her up as they all gang raped her. The head appeared and they let him have his turn with her

15

as they threw money at her. Throwing her purse at her, they tossed her down the stairs.

The boy still sat in the closet as she had said.

It was nighttime and the boy still sat there inside the closet. The boy felt as if he should've stepped out but the sound of desperation in her voice, when she told him not to, convinced him. He felt conflicted once again. Just then there was a noise, someone was coming up the stairs. He looked and saw that it was a woman who went straight to the closet. She opened the door to see him. The boy ducked his head low, so she wouldn't see his face.

He lifted his head up ever so slightly so he could at least get a description of the woman, but she gasped at the sight of his forehead. Not even making it to his face. She grabbed him and went downstairs out of the house, to meet Amy.

"Oh bless you Katlyn," Amy said.

"Amy, whenever I'm out of the house you can call me up anytime." Katlyn said as she ran back in.

The boy saw Amy's face and saw the bruises and gashes that made her face swell. But he could still see her smile, even through all of the scars he could still make out that waring smile.

As she carried him in her arms, walking down the streets unsure of what's next, the boy remembered the money that everyone was throwing at Amy. How all that money had only one place to go, it was with the head. But he also remembered the painful scream she sounded with. "NO!!!!!," she screamed. He thought of stepping back as he did. He thought of the picture he drew back then and he glanced at Amy who was still smiling at him.

The picture, he thought. The I did as he pleased. But how to get past Amy, without putting her in any unnecessary trouble? If he ran, she would surely follow behind him, back into the house, just to take him outside again. He knew she wouldn't put him down or release him. *So what's the use?* he thought. And what of the woman named Katlyn? What is her future?

No, the boy thought, he could do something or at least try to. But what if it didn't work out, and Katlyn went through all that trouble for nothing? Surely the head and delegates had no idea of her actions at all.

She risked her life just to put Amy at ease. The boy felt his crayon and paper. *No it wouldn't be for nothing,* he thought. The boy struggled out of Amy's clutch. He wrote on the paper and left running through the dark thicket. His struggle nudged Amy awake, she yelled out loudly for him but he couldn't hear her anymore. Amy searched the immediate vicinity and found the paper and saw what he wrote: "I'll be back before tomorrow comes."

The boy knew where the house was and stood right in front of it shaking. These men reminded him of the man that did the same thing to him as they did to every victim in this house. The boy's heart pounded furiously as he walked around the house, looking for a point of entry and found a window. He let out a deep breath and jumped for the window. He smashed through the glass which gave him severely deep wounds. The sound of broken glass woke the entire house up.

The delegates ran downstairs checking what the trouble was. "The fuck." one the said. The glass had given the boy lacerations all over his body. He was now bleeding profusely from his wounds.

"I'll beat… beat you all down." the boy could barely say these words out loud.

The men looked at the bloody mess on the floor. The men laughed at him and told the boy to get the fuck out.

"No, I'll beat you all.." the boy said. "S-sorry men." he stammered.

"The fuck did you just say, boy?" one of them said, sounding irritated. "You're about to find out which of us here is real sorry one, you little fuck."

The boy tried to stand but he could barely lift his hands, it was no use. One hit and the boy went down to the ground. He couldn't get up. Several men pinned him down on the ground and beat him mercilessly.

"Holy fuck. Look at his face." one of them cried out. "That ain't no face it's just fucking butchered meat."

The boy was completely at the mercy of the men, they were going to beat him to death.

But the boy was already dead; he died even before the first punch was thrown, dead before he jumped through the glass window and bled out. This boy was already dead the moment he chose this path. He died when he hung himself, accepting defeat. He was now unconscious in the basement as the pictures moved forward, crawling out of the papers.

Putting him in chains with hooks that stabbed their way through his body, as he hung. The little boy was alive and crying out in pain.

"Scream louder, bitch boy," the voice said.

They all gathered around him, jerking themselves as they watched. They all gang raped him continuously. As soon as one was done another would take its place. It was a constant flow, from butt to mouth. The boy was hoisted up vertically, one of the men took out a knife and then castrated him and stabbed at it to make another hole. The boy cried and wailed, an endless amount of people found a new hole to pleasure themselves with. They then hung him at an angle and started filling his mouth. The knife was then getting passed around as they stabbed at the boy creating new love holes all over his body which they immediately filled up.

They started beating him horribly. The boy's skull cracked and this time his whole head caved in. Eventually his entire body became nothing but a smear on the floor. He was still there, completely aware, but unmoving as his mind was broken.

He stared at the portrait of I intensely as he came back. The boy didn't survive the beating, yet here he is, looking at the men who were still beating him. He fought back and upon his gaze they all died, falling to the ground like bees. But at a certain price, he saw himself as the delegates in the house, they were looking like himself. He lunged and violently attacked them as if he were a starved wild animal.

He charged, chewing off their arms and gouging out their eyes. Ripping out guts, he felt every bit of what he did, he was in a way doing it to himself. His body was showing the scars. He was so transfixed by the pain but the loathing which fueled him, made him so lost in this brutality. Without thinking, as if he had known, he went upstairs to the head's office.

All the victims of the head including Katlyn had watched as the boy entered the head's office. Gunshots were heard, as the head fired off shots at the boy. But he continued forward, seeing only himself. With his bare hands he ripped open the head's stomach and ate his intestines.

He then tore the head's flesh off his bones and broke one bone off letting him choke with it. Finally he punched through his chest and squeezed his heart until it exploded. Yet in his vision all he saw was his own meat and mutilated body.

The boy, as if coming back to himself again, saw the mess he had made. He vomited, horrified at the scene he suddenly found himself in the middle of. He took deep breaths, composing himself, but he shook as he saw the head and his anger returned.

He grabbed the head by his head and proceeded to grab the bag of money and opened the door. He stepped down the stairs, blood trailing from both his and the head's body. Everyone saw him, including Zefron who immediately backed off after the boy went berserk.

Everyone looked up at the boy who was descending down the stairs. He was drenched in blood, yet he did seem too unstable, not sure whether to cry or attack again. He dragged the head's mutilated body to the middle of the room and left it there, but kept his grip on the bag of money which he kept dragging out of the house. No one followed him outside. He kept dragging the bag of money until he was back at the park, where he saw poor Amy still wandering through the woods, He could only grunt to get her attention.

She wheeled around to face his direction, her face lit up with both astonishment and fear upon seeing her boy covered in new wounds and lots of blood. He expected her to wail loudly, but all he saw was a great deal of relief in her eyes. She hugged him tightly as she ever could, he could feel her body shake every time she inhaled and exhaled.

The boy had done it, he felt as though he had redeemed himself. Feeling nothing but glory. The truth was, deep inside it didn't feel that way. Whatever happened, he wasn't sure how he did it and the voice, he could hear it again.

"None of what just occurred are you responsible for. You are still that same fuckboy that had given in and bitched out. You are completely incapable of anything. Still lying to yourself that you did all that, I took over, so don't own that shit. Lying to yourself that you're still worth something."

The boy looked up at Amy's smile, how bright and warm it was, *she thought something of me however right or wrong, she did,* he thought.

2

The boy sat in his room reading and occasionally taking a peek outside. He did enjoy watching what happened outside, but when he heard Amy communicating to Katlyn in a low voice, they seemed very serious. Amy then opened the door and Katlyn came in.

"Please Amy, just for a moment, That's all I'm asking, girl." Katlyn said.

"I know,I trust you." Amy said.

She left the room, giving one last worrying look at the boy before walking out and closing the door. "Now, can you tell me your name." she said.

She sat down on the floor right alongside him. She looked completely kind and at the same time worried.

"K." the boy said.

"Why did you choose that name, sweetie?" She asked.

"It just fits, I guess. Simple." he could try to tell her but at this point he really saw no need to do so. He felt a change within himself so he decided that he should have a name he chose for himself, like it was needed.

The boy somehow looked uneasy with her presence, but he knew she was one of the good people.

"Now, can you tell me what happened on the night Amy took you from the house?" she said, sitting beside him.

"I don't really remember much from that night." he said. He started to cry, as he knew he would.

Katlyn hugged him tight to comfort him. "It's fine, darling. It's fine." she said. "Amy would like to call you something different." Katlyn said.

"She'd like to call you Danny or Danielle." she continued. "Let's go with that, at least for now."

Amy walked into the room and could sense the boy shaking. She could sense it a lot now as he always shook. Amy stepped out and he stopped shaking.

"Are you okay Danielle?" she said as he ran to her.

"We best get moving now." Katlyn said.

Later, they were down a road heading to a hotel while the boy slept in the backseat. Katlyn was in the front seat while Amy was driving the car.

"Amy, you had to have seen it for yourself right?" Katlyn said, "How he was almost like a different person. I mean, he got to that money somehow."

Amy was hesitant to speak, but she eventually did.

"I saw him bleed all over." she said. "How he should have died when I first got him and how little and fragile he was." she said, fighting back tears. "And now, even after all that, it's still not over."

"Zefron had a good thing going for him back at the head's place. Even having his own operation going on and how he would cut deals with us behind his back, you knew that. And now that he's built his business up again, he will be coming for the boy and everyone within his radius." Katlyn explained.

"That's what he said before I ran away and escaped." Amy said, nervously.

"Katlyn, thanks for everything. You, coming here and informing us and not going away." Amy said.

"Well, you're more of a sister to me than anyone in my family, and besides he knows about you and the boy, plus me with association. I'd be fucked even if I wanted to ditch you." she joked.

Amy kept looking back at the boy. He was shaking again. Amy's hands tightened on the wheel. Katlyn looked at Amy growing all the more uneasy. She put her hand on her shoulder, "Amy, it's gonna get better." she said.

Katlyn was there when that horrible abortion happened, she tried to intervene but was backhanded by one of the delegates then they locked her in a room. In that locked room all she could do was pound on the door pointlessly. She could hear Amy shouting maniacally from all the pain and grief.

That was a frightening time and how savage the head was, along with his delegates. Amy suddenly swerved on the road, almost hitting a car. She jolted up at the sight of it along with Katlyn. Katlyn then offered to take control of the wheel and Amy agreed.

Amy however, sat in the backseat along with the boy. Holding him to her and not taking an eye off him. Katlyn looked at the rearview mirror and wondered if it made her a horrible person to think this might be a growing problem that's unhealthy for Amy.

She saw how attached she was to the boy, almost like an obsession. How she would forget about everything else when it came to him. Definitely another time to talk about it though, she erased the thought from her mind as she tried to concentrate on the road.

The boy however was still shaking as he was once again lost in his own consciousness, dreaming of the crossed eyed people again and how they brutalized him.

His tears streamed from his face as he found himself to be stripped off of his appendages again. Wrapped in chains again; only this time he was used as a human toilet and ate the waste from their bodies. The chains however felt different as he could feel spikes dig into his flesh and tear at it with every movement he made.

He could hear the tearing of his flesh as they continued to inflict every form of torture unto him. He felt as if he was there stuck in that dark basement forever. It was as if they were actually performing every torture and death that existed on him and made it worse. The boy knew this, somehow, someway he knew this, and yet he didn't know why.

It was as if he never left, like he's been there as far as he could remember. He tried to remember something else, but this was all that there was. Him beaten and assaulted in every way possible. Killed more times than he could remember, assaulted many times, beaten and bludgeoned to the extremes. This is the utmost pain he had endured; this was the pain he knew for centuries.

That's what it felt like, he knew he had not been here for centuries and it would not stop. Every type of death played in history or type of torture that had ever been done he had experienced it, without reason he knew this. They hung him up on a tree and this was where he was exposed to the coldest winter, and the hottest summer, the worst storms and the most savage hurricanes to have ever occurred.

Eventually the rope tore and he drifted off into the flood drowning forever. Until the flood went away and he awoke from his dream. The boy stared from the backseat of the car to the front seat in total shock of what just occurred to him.

"Danny." Amy said.

The boy looked up in response and saw that it was her. He leaned back and relaxed slightly. This was to put Amy further at ease. Then she saw the marks forming up again, the scars coming forward like before on that fateful night.

"Katlyn, he's bleeding again." Amy said, her voice trembling.

Katlyn pulled over at the side of the road, she looked over to see what was going on.

"My God." she said out loud.

The boy's flesh was being peeled back. You could see his bone, it was as if he was being turned inside out. The boy almost fainted from the sight and with the unbearable pain, he could only look at Amy.

"Danny, stay with me." Amy said, staring straight at him.

She held onto him soaking herself with blood as well. The boy tightly hugged her as if this was the only way to survive this moment.

"Alright, you said that this has happened several times now and he always turned out alright." Katlyn said, still trying to be rational.

"Yes, that's right." Amy answered trying to compose herself with that thought.

"Yeah, he always turns out alright in the end. No matter what, he always does." she said, repeating it to herself.

They sat there for a while watching him bleed. His flesh moving and tearing almost like it had a mind of its own. Amy whimpered as she held him tighter with each passing moment. When it finally seems to have stopped, the boy was back to the way he was before his flesh crawled. The inside of the car was a bloody mess, with Amy colored with the boy's crimson blood.

Katlyn let out a big sigh; she started up the car and continued driving. The boy still hung onto Amy, with her rubbing his head for reassurance.

There was no way they could pass at a motel with Amy along with the boy and the interior of the car a bloody mess. They do have some spare clothes but what do they have to use to wash the blood off within the car though. These thoughts passed Katlyn's mind as she drove down the road nearing a store.

Finally. she thought. She parked the car a ways off from the store.

"Alright, Amy. I'll be back in a minute." she said. "Is there anything you might want?"

"No, Katlyn. I'm fine." Amy responded

"What about Danny?" Katlyn asked, looking at him.

"He's got food. I made sure of that before we left." Amy assured her.

"Alright, then." Katlyn said as she headed out of the car.

Huh, she's just like me. No family, no friends other than me. Amy thought. She remembered Katlyn telling her this. *We really are on our own, however desperate these times seem to get, it's still worth not being under the head anymore.*

Though he did provide food, water, shelter, and comfort. All that came with the price of the oppression that he brought with it. *This is what I prefer,* she thought. She looked at the boy and wondered deeply. Katlyn said that she had seen it herself, how he viciously attacked the delegates and how he killed the head.

Was this little boy really capable of such a thing? How is it that he gets these wounds out of nowhere and has these moments. Instances like these is where you think God himself hates him. How else could you explain that? What was going on with this boy?

She tried to contact a doctor but just couldn't trust them. At least not in the town they had just left. Everyone in there seems to be under at least some influence from Zefron.

When I saw you with that big bag of cash later that same night, it happened for the first time and then again and again, all in that same night. For no reason the horrible things happened to you Danny. You losing limbs, skin being burned and decayed, I saw how your body would twist in pain.

Amy erased the thoughts from her mind.

But you always come out fine in the end like nothing ever happened. Katlyn didn't know how she had gotten wrapped up in all of this. Too late to turn around now though, she thought.

Just that moment she saw Katlyn running back with water and towels.

"Here." she said. "Wet them, clean yourselves and change clothes." She looked as if she was in a hurry, frightened really.

"Katlyn is something wrong?" Amy said worryingly.

"Amy, I saw one of the delegates that was from Zefron's new fit." Katlyn whispered.

"What?" Amy shouted, suddenly spooking the boy.

"Yeah, just can't seem to shake em. It's not even a week and Zefron seems to have things spread further out than usual." Katlyn said.

"Are you sure it was them? Like, they're still working for him." Amy said

"Well, judging from the way that truck is coming up. I'd say that looks pretty familiar." Katlyn said as she started the car.

Amy looked at the rear and saw the truck coming up fast.

"We're not going to be able to get away in this car." Katlyn said.

"They're about to ram us." Amy said looking behind.

"Hold onto something then." Katlyn said.

She held the boy close to her and braced for it. It only took one hit from the truck to drive them off the road. Katlyn tried to keep the car straight but eventually lost control and rolled over into a ditch. Amy then saw her vision fade to black as she felt the boy still around her arm but she couldn't turn her neck. Something was blocking it. She could only stare at Katlyn's body not knowing if she was dead or alive.

Amy woke up to Katlyn strapped in a chair right next to her. She sees Danny strapped as well and sitting right behind him is Zefron who is smiling at him. Around the room there were several women and men, *His delegates* she thought.

Zefron took the boy from the seat and bent him over the table. Danny tried to fight but Zefron proved to be too strong for the fragile boy. He is then strapped to the table.

Amy tries to sit up but several others hold her down as well.

"Amy, wait." Katlyn said, she gestured her head at a gun that they held up to the boy's head.

A woman showed up and sat on a couch directly in front of the boy and spread her legs wide.

"So boy, I saw what you did to all those delegates back at the house and what you did to the head. You probably thought that was it, right?" Zefron said.

Zefron unbuckled his pants. "You proved that you were willing and that's all it took, right? Well, let me tell you something." he leaned over and spoke in his ear. "Cut the head off a snake and another one will grow."

"You see, when it comes to power, someone who is a threat eventually comes around and takes over. Eventually there comes a time when someone challenges the ruler. They take aim at each other and in the end the bigger, better one wins." Zefron said. "This is me asserting that notion."

The woman began touching herself and the boy looked at a mirror that showed Amy's and Katlyn's reflection but more importantly, their reflections. Amy's in tears, while Katlyn's in shock. Zefron then thrusts inside him as the woman continues to touch herself.

He got rougher as the woman began to climax, moaning sweetly as a result. Amy began going hysterical as Zefron laughed at it all. Katlyn was distraught.

Zefron eventually finished and hoisted up his pants, then Katlyn and Amy were then taken away while the gun was still being held at the boy's head. Amy tried her best to compose herself while they were both forced into a cage.

They were then wheeled outside into a wooden area. Katlyn tried her best to comfort a crying Amy while they took them further into the woods. The delegates then grabbed wooden spears and surrounded the cage.

"Wha- What's going on?" Katlyn said.

They then took the wheels off and now the cage was stationary. Amy looked up and saw what was happening.

"Zefron wanted to make sure that you knew this was his idea." One then stabbed at Katlyn's leg.

"Unnngggh!" Katlyn howled in pain.

"No!" Amy screamed.

They all then surrounded the cage getting even more closer. " Let them have it!" one roared.

Amy, as if instinctively, covered herself over Katlyn. Taking most of the stabbing.

"Amy! What are you doing?" Katlyn asked.

Amy didn't respond; instead she just stayed on top of her, forcing her down.

"Fine by me." one of the delegates said. "Keep going, focus on the red head!!!!."

They all then continuously stabbed at her, making her drip blood. One stabbed at her and got the stick stuck in her hip. The delegate twisted and pulled hard until he got his stick back.

This however was being videotaped and the boy was forced to watch along with Zefron who was grinning still.

Another stabbed at her and Amy caught the stick and broke it in half.

"Oh, so you're tough now, eh?" one of the delegates said.

They continued to stab her repeatedly. She noticed how they weren't paying attention to Katlyn now. Amy couldn't think of a way to get out of the cage, she looked around furiously. Another suddenly stabbed at her throat making her gurgle on blood, and another thrusted the stick just below her lungs.

She grew tired of thinking, with a jolt of energy rushing through her, she panicked, ran and charged at the cage.

"Oh she's fighting back now." one of them said.

She backed up and did it again. As she backed up attempting for the third time, one of the delegates timed it just right and got her in the torso as she was charging.

She was breathing heavily, the air she breathed came through her torso and let out through the hole in her throat. The loose skin that hung from her throat flapped as she took heavy labored breaths.

They all mocked her because of the skin that hung from her torso. It was big enough to cover her face. *They think this is a game. They hurt my friend and hurt my boy.*

"You hurt my boy." she exclaimed louder. She grew angry from fear and slowly, blind rage slowly consumed her. She ripped and ate the flesh hanging from her torso, and stared at them.

They stared back in awe and decided it was time to end this. They continuously barraged her with stabs as she continuously charged the cage.

"Die, you fucking pig!" one cried out.

Still she continued to charge the cage. Suddenly the cage gave way a little and what she did; it was working.

Katlyn tried to get up but Amy knocked her back down to stop her. Katlyn stared at her.

Amy, she thought. *Of course, the boy and me. That's easy to understand but Amy, look at what you're doing to yourself.*

They continued as she was relentless and kept on charging at the cage. The cage in turn was getting weaker. Amy, now barely being able to stand charged once more. The cage now seemed fragile. One of the delegates stabbed at her jaw. Amy fell to the ground in a bloody mess. From where she lay, she immediately stood up and continued to target the part of the cage where she kept charging.

"No fucking way." one of them said.

Amy, shaking with adrenaline, stood up and charged once more; the cage door flew open. She was able to get back to her feet before the adrenaline in her body gave out, making her collapse from exhaustion.

Zefron stared at the monitor, he then radioed to the team in the woods.

"Alright, haul them back into the guest room." one of the delegates said.

"That was a spectacle indeed." Zefron said. "She actually broke through the cage. She most likely will die as a result of this." he said with a smile on his face.

"But that inspired me so much that I would want to keep doing this." He said as his smile grew bigger and menacing. "Torturing them continuously, torturing you continuously to the point of insanity until your body gives out and can no longer go on."

"I want to give you something worse than hell itself. I want you to have a new meaning for pain and you will learn to fear my name." he proclaimed.

He then pulled out a needle and went to inject the boy with whatever was in it. That's when Katlyn and Amy were wheeled in the room to witness what would happen next.

When everyone left the room including Zefron, that's when the restraints came off from their chairs. Amy then ran to her boy and grabbed him but as soon as she touched him, he started to twitch and go into a seizure.

As she continued to touch him, he only got worse. Katlyn seemed to have noticed this and she went for Amy.

"Amy, wait." she said. "It's only happening when you touch him." She grabbed her and pulled her away from him.

"What?" Amy cried out. She then looked to her boy and held her head as she sank down to her knees.

She couldn't even touch her boy, not only that but she was responsible for this: his suffering was her fault. Katlyn came over to comfort her, wrapping her arms around her as they both could only watch.

An hour passed by and now it seemed that the boy had completely passed out from the seizure. Amy somehow was completely unsure if it was safe to touch him. Katlyn stared at Amy who seemed to be considering trying to touch him.

Then the boy started writhing again but this time, it was different. His bones started cracking and blood coming out from his pores. His bones then punctured through his skin. His eyes were pouring out blood.

It was a terrifying sight, the boy was experiencing pain on a completely different level than how it looked. He is in his lost consciousness state again.

It seemed that the boy found himself in space and floating along in it's empty depth. As a rising feeling grew within his chest, it slowly spread across his body. The feeling was of something warm. He was heading towards the sun.

He looked around and saw that there were smaller stars that surrounded him. His body split into smaller pieces, being reduced to the smallest unit and spread throughout the space. He however still maintained his consciousness.

He somehow could see everything, even though his body was completely scattered into atoms. Still somehow, he retained his consciousness and looked at all the pieces of his body headed to the stars. The heat soon turned from warm to blazing hot. He somehow could still feel the heat, like he was still heading towards the sun and now he was inside it. When all his pieces went to their separate stars, the stars and including the sun all combined. The heat was unbearable and pain immeasurable.

The giant star that was made up of all the other stars exploded, and the heat and pain magnified ridiculously.

A black hole was formed and he suffered all from what it offered to him.

He then woke up still floating in the ocean, the sky he could see was filled with stars shooting from one point. However his vision faded as was his hearing: he had completely lost all hearing and vision.

He then felt the waves grow more violent and rapid in their movement. He was in the middle of a hurricane and next he was in the middle of the ocean. The waves picked him up and smashed him down back into the ocean.

This continued for several hours; the waves were showing no mercy. Even struck and electrocuted by lightning so many times it felt like it was one continuous lighting bolt.

He felt it and it was the most powerful bolt to ever hit. This was magnified with every time he was hit. Eventually the hurricane subsided but the pain wouldn't go away in fact it only grew more and more each moment.

The pain spike was astoundingly high. The pain he felt one second felt like a paradise after the next second hit. The pain spike grew higher and higher with every second and now it was as if it was happening faster and faster now, feeling the spike in less than a second.

Everything hurt him from contact to just thought; everything caused him unrelenting suffering. He however felt something touch him drag him somewhere, then he woke up.

The boy found himself looking back at Amy and Katlyn again; he was out of his lost state again, but the pain was still there and still growing.

Zefron then showed up in the room shocked and curiosity filled his face at what he had just seen on the camera. *The boy was as if being crushed by an invisible force, like it's body was destroying itself,* he thought.

And just then he saw the boy being put back together again. *This was definitely something on another level indeed,* he thought. He then walked over to the boy and saw him face to face.

He could see himself, losing his way several times now. It was clear as day, but he still got himself back on track, he thought. Lying to himself gave himself false hope. He noticed the child could not see anymore.

He snapped at his ear and the boy responded.

"I have an out for you boy." Zefron said, grinning. "If you can fight these delegates then I'll let you all go with no trouble and you won't see my face again."

"Make some sound if you're willing to do it."

The boy groaned.

"Good enough." Zefron said as he exited the room.

Amy and Katlyn were taken to a glass room where they could see the boy.

"If you step outside this room, the boy will receive electric shocks that will cause him to go into a seizure even worse than what you saw earlier." Zefron said with a smile.

He exited the room and went and sat in another where he could see Amy and Katlyn as well as the boy along with his henchmen that just entered the room, and they all could see him back.

The delegates entered the room and started surrounding the boy. One of them as instructed, snapped at the boy's ear, this time he didn't respond. He could no longer hear. Zefron started laughing. He then soon gave them the signal to assault. The delegates then began to attack.

The boy now who was completely in the dark, could only feel kicking, punching, and stomping all over his body.

"Hey, bitch boy."

The boy was stunned at what he heard, then instantly knew who it was. The same one who killed all those delegates before, it was the I.

Now somewhere else, he saw himself surrounded by a crowd and this crowd went as far as his eyes could see. They were all around him. They stared at him in fear. He went to assault them all, tearing them limb from limb, eating others whole and while ripping the others inside out. He felt every bit of what his victims were but more.

Eventually the crowd turned into a huge pile of mutilated bodies. And the boy suffered from every wound that he gave to them but felt worse than that.

The boy felt his blood dripping again. He was bleeding all over his body and could see everything. He felt himself at a higher consciousness. He saw the presence of every delegate in the room and by the simple thought of it, they all collapsed down dead.

Amy and Katlyn both looked up shocked by what they just saw. Zefron however, was still grinning and completely absorbed in the scene he was witnessing.

The boy however understood it all now. He saw that his will was against everyone in the room. The pain he felt spiked more ferociously, giving them all but just a small fraction of the pain he felt.

They all then gave in to him taking their lives. Once the pain became too great to bear. He felt them all however. All the delegates he killed and the cross-eyed people. They all began their assault on him in his mind.

He felt every bit of the ceaseless beating they were giving him in his mind. He tried to center himself to where he was. He felt blood oozing down his arms, pouring over his face.

"What the fuck just happened?" Katlyn said.

"They're all dead." Amy said.

Amy looked at the boy with both relief and disbelief at what she had seen. Katlyn then looked at Zefron who seemed to be getting up from his chair.

He held a remote.

"Wait, what's he holding in his hand?" Katlyn said.

Amy turned to him as he clicked the button. The boy started to writhe in pain, having a seizure, while being electrocuted.

Zefron looked at the boy to see what would happen. The boy then stopped moving, stood up and now walked to the window where Zefron was. *I'm losing myself,* Zefron thought. *The boy can somehow notice where I am even though he's still both blind and deaf.*

They both stared at each other through the glass. Amy got up and ran out of the room. Katlyn grabbed her arm.

"The boy will be getting shocked again." she said.

"Look at him." Amy pleaded.

Katlyn then glanced at the boy, the way his body moved and twitched.

The boy was still getting electrocuted now. Katlyn already knew this but still tried to stop her.

"No! Amy!" Katlyn yelled.

As soon as Amy touched him, she was electrocuted as well. She then collapsed back on the floor, however still conscious thanks to the adrenaline going through her.

"Well, look at this. The same little fuck that somehow took out everybody in the mansion, makes an appearance again." Zefron said.

Katlyn went to Amy who was still dazed by the shock and then looked to where Zefron and the boy were staring at each other.

"Well, till next time then." he said.

There was a little slot in the glass window where Zefron pushed a small ticket through. The boy caught it as the wind guided the piece of paper toward him.

Zefron pressed the button on the remote again. That's when he noticed that it was out of battery, the remote was already dead from the settings being on max for so long. He then walked off into another room, glancing at both Amy and Katlyn.

For a woman to survive a shock of that magnitude and that boy, that small boy, he thought to himself, eventually cracking a smile. *This is all too great to be true, I'm going to milk this for as long as I can.*

Seeing that kid, who would think that he could throw a cranny in my operations. Seeing the fear in his eyes, his pain and regret, he said to himself. *Ah, what a rush it was to see. I want to see that again, more of it.*

've never seen anything like this one of a kind soul. I hope he keeps posting up and accepts that ticket I've given him. I would enjoy seeing more of him.

"All of this really is coming together quite nicely." he said. Zefron then started to sweat at the very thought of it.

They all are nothing but play toys at my disposal, just another piece in my toybox.

3

Amy was fast asleep from the pills she took. Katlyn looked at her worryingly as she heard the door creak open: the boy stepped out. Katlyn couldn't even face him, out of disappointment to herself.

How could I have done this to you, she thought.

She felt bad for doing this without Amy knowing but it felt like it was the best she could do. The boy continued out into the open road where it soon led into an open alley. The boy was bruised badly earlier this morning and would definitely have it worse tonight after this.

There was a door that led the boy inside where a crowd was surrounding a cage. They all roared at the sight of him, one wolf whistled. In the crowd the boy could see men and women, as well as little kids his age.

As the boy stepped into the cage, he saw a big man who sat on a stool on the other side of the cage and looked back at him with great anticipation. There was the ding of the bell and with that, the fight began.

When the boy went to raise his fist to hit the man, his opponent only laughed at him and he struck the boy down with one hit. Then the man kept beating the boy until he was bloody and old wounds reopened from his last fight.

The bell rang and the boy was completely dazed. The man pulled down his pants as well as pulled down the boy's shorts. The crowd cheered as the man had his way with the boy. This was one of the rules of the cage fight. The loser would be fucked by the winner, it was said just before you enter the cage. The man finally ejaculated on his back.

The boy then stood up and went directly to the house where Katlyn waited for him. Just like that, he got beaten, got fucked and walked back to rinse and repeat. She cleaned him and treated his wounds and finally laid him down to rest. He has another fight just past midnight so he would have to get some sleep while he could.

Katlyn however could not sleep. *How did things get this bad? To where Zefron would always know where we were and how he tortured us like this. This was the only way to ensure he wouldn't hurt any of us or kill Amy.*

All he wanted in return was for the boy to fight, hence the ticket. The boy had to get to where most of his delegates were. She tried to get Amy and the boy and run but Zefron found them again. Surprisingly, the boy agreed, she was puzzled as to why he would do that. She thought she knew the obvious reason which was most likely because of her and Amy's safety.

But she felt there was more to it as well.

Whatever the case she couldn't let Amy know and as much as she was afraid to admit it, the woman just wasn't sane anymore.

As time went on, not a single word was said between Katlyn and the boy. Amy eventually slipped into a coma from the pills given to her to keep her asleep. It was much easier, that way, she wouldn't go into a manic state. The boy continued with the fights not winning a single one of them.

The strong takes advantage of the weak, that phrase was all that went through his mind. That thought burned its way into his head and that's when he heard the voice again.

"I can give you what you want, boy." the voice said. *It's the I,* the boy thought. "I love seeing you squirm though. I can help you out, boy."

The boy still had that growing pain and his mind being constantly attacked; he saw himself being brutalized constantly in that basement. It felt like he never escaped, he still saw them finding new ways to torture him and brutalize him.

All these things never escaped him; that's all that filled his vision along with what was going on around him. The next fight however, he won. Then the next one and then one after that. Time had passed and now the boy was older and had gotten better at cage fighting. Now a man, he was young and built up quite nice, from his own training regime. He then named himself K.

His next fight was up and it was against a man that was a pretty scary individual, but the boy who was now a man had not lost in a while so he should feel pretty confident about this. But he wasn't.

The bell rang and K threw a punch, but the man caught it easily. *What? what's going on?* K thought.

"See? I told you I would help you out but like I said, there are moments where I love seeing you squirm."

K then threw another punch, and the man caught both of them. Finally he grabbed K and kissed him before slamming him into the cage.

"I'm gonna enjoy having you, boy." the man said.

K felt scared and angry towards himself again. *What a familiar feeling.*

He ran to the man trying to punch him again, but the man grabbed him and slammed him to the ground and started spanking him. Finally the man started ferociously beating him until the bell rang.

The man then dragged K to another room, threw him onto the bed and made sure that the cameras were rolling. He saw the crowd of people watch him as he tore K's pants off. He felt every inch of K's body.

"You know, you've got a fucking hard ass body, boy." he breathed into his ears.

Then he rubbed K's ass as he fingered it. Then he grabbed K's shoulders and rammed his entire dick in.

The man heard K moan intensely as he went faster and faster in his rhythm. The man was living the dream. The way the ass bounced like a shockwave was addicting to him. He became lost in it. The sounds K made in response to his thrusts was like a sweet melody.

He turned K over and opened his legs wide and thrust himself into him again. He then picked him up. While still holding K up, he started fucking him against the wall. He looked into his eyes and K was forced to look into his.

The man kissed him, shoving his tongue down his throat, biting his lips and his neck.

K's moans grew louder and this only motivated him more. Slamming him on the bed, he turned him on his side, lifted his leg and continued thrusting.

Finally, he turned him over and lifted his hips up, doggy-style and thrusted even harder. The pounding noise was extremely loud. The whole bed was shaking as the man grabbed K's head smothering it into the covers. His grip on him tightened, his nails eventually digging into his skin causing K to bleed.

The man then took K's head and forced his dick into his mouth. The gagging sound as the man forcefully took control of K's head as thrusted into his mouth was addicting. Slapping K repeatedly, he then pinned him down on the concrete ground.

Laying on top of him he continued to pound him until he came inside of him. K felt the warm liquid make its way inside of him as well. He felt the man's heavy breath as he lay over him.

"I think I'm in love with you, boy." the man said.

Later that night he stalked him as he went home, and K knew he was watching. Right when K opened the door, he heard the man blow a whistle at him. As usual, Katlyn never talked to K as K never talked to her.

K however did go to see Amy and wondered if she would ever wake up. It filled his mind along with everything else, everyday it did.

As the nightmares took ahold of him again, constantly seeing the crossed-eyed people torture him. The never ending pain grew inside of him, his mind was assaulted every second. He looked out the window.

The man stood smiling at him, blowing kisses to him. K decided to go outside and try to settle this once again. Katlyn was fast asleep so she wouldn't be bothered anyway. K went to him to try and fight him, but the man beat him down severely.

He then dragged him inside and closed the door behind him.

"Hey, this is a nice place" he said. "You know that video I have of you? It's blowing up all over the internet. People can't get enough of it. Can't blame 'em, either. That shit was hot." he said.

The man started walking around the house like he owned it. This made K furious, flashbacks of the man that used to act just like this came rushing back at him.

"You know, I just can't help but see you like this." the man said.

He suddenly started choking K until he passed out.

K awoke in a hospital bed with someone sitting beside him. A man smiling as he awoke.

"Hey, how's it going there?" he said.

K remained silent.

"So, I just happened to see you out there floating in the sea. You seem a little lost. My name's Joseph by the way." he said. "Don't worry. I'll be with you every step of the way for this." he said comfortingly.

"After all, that's why I'm here." he said as he clapped his hands.

K found himself in a wheelchair, missing all his appendages. Someone was wheeling him around; he looked and saw it was Joseph. Everything around him was black and he could see something that looked like tall boulders with words carved inside of them.

As he passed by them he found that they were easy to read.

"Think of these as laws." Joseph said. "This is the constant on how things always operate, you made them yourself."

"The growing pain with no limit, forever spiking to make the last second seem like a relief to what you always feel now. This pain in both mind and body, and everything else in between."

"One will against many oppositions, your will against others."

"This right here K, means that you and whoever it is that you are against, will feel a certain level of pain. As you both fight, the pain increases until someone quits. That's how you were able to defeat those delegates in that chamber. However, the dreaded reality is that they can only feel an insanely small fraction of what you feel." he explained.

"Also this does not halt that same ceaseless pain that you are feeling right now. It's a constant that when fighting, you fight all the way to sleep."

"When brutalized enough, the K factor will be at your will?"

"Yes. So, the K factor, you can think of it as a way out always and completely competent in every situation. No matter what the circumstances are, you will be able to do anything you wish. Effectively making you a god in a sense. You think it, and it happens at your will."

"However, this can only be done so long as you take a heavy amount of punishment. Spike your pain significantly up to where you can automatically get this with your own will." he explained.

"Torment in the mind, forever and always."

"This states that whatever is going on psychologically in your head, as you may have noticed. You constantly see yourself in the basement with those crossed-eyed people or any other person that comes to your imagination. Being brutalized in every way one can imagine." he said.d

"This is like another reality that stays with you. You can still be aware of yourself and what you're doing. It's like brushing teeth or eating but consciously, it's like you are still there and never left. Think of yourself to be in both worlds at the same time."

"Constantly attacking oneself, brutal in fashion as his anger relentlessly rises."

"Now, remember the part where you are in both worlds. Well this is another that has been created by you. In this one you brutalize yourself, one of your fantasies?" he added.

"Obviously as you continue, you will find more and more things to be added. But for now this is all that I can show. You will find yourself in other worlds that you created randomly. This in time, you will learn to control as well. I'm about to send you back now, brace yourself." he said.

The heavy dreadful rustling of chains could be heard in the far distance. These chains were buried deep into the man's flesh. The flesh had actually grown over the old rusted chains as a result of how long they've been there. The chains burden him, greatly limiting his range of motion and making each movement harder than the last.

He was a sight of a swollen mass of infected and diseased meat. Puss excreted from his pore, skin black in some parts clearly showing the area of his body that's already dead. Other parts were green showing the area of the infection or virus; the rest however were red from the blood that oozed and squirted out from his body.

In fact, the whole field he hand-made alone was made entirely colored in crimson just by his knees dragging along the land. His knees however, seemed no more as they have been grinded down due to the constant grinding of earth on them. He was now at his waist.

This man had given himself a task that had to be done and completed. *It was what they all deserved*, he thought.

The man had been working for a long time now. Years have passed by for sure, decades went and more centuries flew by. The man however didn't pay attention to the time elapsing but the people, men, women, and children that he would be laying to rest.

He could see the remains of every individual that lay underground, both animal and human. He would dig them out with his bare hands. At times, flesh seemed to be on them but other times he would be carrying out a skeleton. He knew who this person was, what this individual did and the life they lived.

There was a huge heap of stone that grew from the ground tall and big. This is what he used for his tombstone. He'd smash the rocks by balling up the dangling chains in his hand and striking, carving the stone. Soon enough he could tell that his hand seemed to be dented in and missing some flesh. This came from the constant rough handling of stone and metal. Adding to the weight of the chains, the stone weighed him down as he journeyed the long path back to the cemetery.

Funny enough that there was always stone. A mound of stone would always be somewhere and right when there seemed to be just too little.

Another large mound would appear within sight of the other one. This was all too convenient, almost seeming like some force was at work.

This however did not bother the man at all for he had a task he was too focused to worry about anything else. He would not stop until this job was done.

The man, who was now dragging himself along to the cemetery, had no waist. Only from the chest up and arms, crawling with the stone he had carved. It was a long path from where he was to the cemetery; this was due to how he felt that it should be a cemetery completely undisturbed by his work. The two were in completely separate locations beyond the sight of the eye. This was to be a place completely cut off from anything unnatural, like his workspace of sorts, where he makes the tombstones.

As he continued to crawl, the chains now covered in dried blood, pulled on his flesh and tore it apart. Friction caused the chains to come off at some parts and be dragged along the ground from his rotting body.

The man with the final tombstone had crawled in and laid the final one to rest but he did not stop there. He continued with every creature that lived and stepped foot on the land he was on. He would not stop until he was finished.

One would think that he couldn't possibly accomplish it, as it was downright impossible. Especially considering the state that he's in, the speed at which he was going, all the chains and the stone weighing him down. This just couldn't be done, it won't be done. He literally is making graves at a much slower rate than ones that were dying.

He eventually did do it, finally taking up all the land, one flat field. The only thing left that was not taken up was the workspace that had been cut off from the cemetery. This he dug up and buried. The graveyard was not only to the humans or creatures but to every plant and microorganism as well. The man quite literally took into account every single life that inhabited the land.

The entire land was covered in blood. Looking at it now, it seemed like some kind of memorial. A tribute to the people that gave him something. He did not want his workspace to be a part of this. This belonged to them and them only.

However, he was not finished as he dug around and around the land. In his weakened state, every movement was painful and agonizing. He dug and dug, digging around the land, he was to make sure that his land wouldn't be tampered with and that it would remain in sight to marvel at but not disturbed. He dug underground and eventually hit water. With him digging in the water at the muddy foundation, he wore the land away.

The memorial broke away from the land and set to sea, becoming its own. Yet he continued digging away at the edges until the memorial was in one complete circle. It was at this point that his hands were no more. He continued to scrape at the land with just his arms, which eventually wore down to his elbows. When he could no longer use his arms he used his head. It was then at long last that he finally set the island onto the ocean and built its base from the ocean floor up so it would not be destroyed by the water.

He gazed upon the memorial as he floated away on the ocean surface. The blood that stained the land looked as if covering it in its entirety. *Ah yes,* he thought. The Crimson Memorial. Birds could be seen from above and ate at him, eating out both of his eyes. However they left him alone after some time.

He could feel something crawl into his ear and something made its way into his head from the eye sockets. Soon he could neither hear. He only could feel the calmness of the waves as he floated. Oh, it was too great, just to feel the soothing water take him and carry him on. The sun was bearing down on him and it only added satisfaction to the tranquility that he was in. He could stay here for a long time but the pain was still there and it would always stay there. He knew it somehow. Only then did he notice all the chains were torn away from his body. This was probably due to him working and time passing by which weakened the chains and made them come off.

The water felt very wavy and became very wild. He felt the water fly into the air, sweeping him along with it and smashing him into the ocean. The ocean pushed and shoved him. *Wow, the water is being quite the bully today,* he thought. His body was lifted again and thrown deep under water. *This is sort of scary and fun at the same time,* he thought.

He floated back up and would be at the mercy of the storm again. It was cold and wet fun but not enough to make him disdain. He was being thrown around the ocean and smashed by the waves. This continued for hours on end.

The storm eventually went away and soon the water was calm again. Decades would go by with him just floating aimlessly on the ocean surface. Of course a storm would come to throw him around, at times it would be wild and unrelenting, other times it would be quite mild.

He felt something grab and drag him, then he felt a hard surface beneath him. Things were touching him, picking him up and placing him down on something soft. After a minute or so, he felt a movement like he was being carried.

K then found himself on the bed facedown. With his arms tied up, the man was fucking him again. When he finished, he threw K off the bed and saw that he was conscious again.

The man grinned. "You know, I think you have a knack for coming into this kind of trouble." he said. "It seemed to me like you never really had a break from any of this. From what some of the other guys from Zefron told me, you've been having trouble since the get go." he said.

"Well tell me, sweetie. Ya do like this shit, huh?" he said as he slapped him. "Do you like what happens to you? you sick fuck." he slapped K again.

K then saw Katlyn creep up behind him with a lamp and smashed it across his head.

The man fell over and Katlyn rushed to K to try and untie him. The man, still a little dazed, sees Katlyn and grabs her by the head and yanks her to his face.

"Funny seeing you here, girl. You've become quite famous since you last left. Hey, if you're here then that means that she's also here, right?"

The man then threw her to K and began looking around the house for her. "Oh man, wait until I see her." he said. Katlyn then got up and went after him but he backhanded her away. Taking no interest in her as a potential threat; he searched the house for Amy. Katlyn then stumbled into the kitchen and grabbed a knife.

She walked behind him quietly then lunged and stabbed him repeatedly until he went down. Committing to the action now, she then kept stabbing until she's out of breath. She's covered in blood staring off into space, still absorbed by the shock but eventually looks at her hands.

In the other room, K was still trying to escape the ropes and did so thanks to Katlyn loosening it for him. As he gets up, Katlyn appears in the room in tears, hugs K.

"I'm sorry boy for everything. I'm sorry I let this happen." she said.

Later that day Katlyn went to wash herself and the both of them along with Amy left the house and never looked back.

4

K sat bloodsoaked on the couch as Katlyn tended to Amy right beside him. Katlyn at first tried to remedy whatever was happening to K every time his body started acting weird. After a while it was no use and with this happening almost all day everyday. She went from looking the other way, to sitting right beside him when it happened. She'd been desensitized to it. Although she hoped this would eventually lead to something more as time went on. As a human being she had to admit that she was pathetic.

Seeing the young boy in pain brought Katlyn satisfaction. Especially after the misfortune he brought Amy, it came to the point where she was driven to insanity, a coma resulting from the pills that she was taking. This made her hatred toward the boy grow only worse. She thought of killing him but how would she explain that to Amy. She thought of running away but Amy would want to find him. She thought of just killing both the boy and Amy, thinking that would be a better fate, but quickly dismissed the idea as that wasn't an idea she was too fond of, but still an idea. That all depended on whether Amy would ever wake up.

Two months have passed and now it seems that they have grown at least somewhat comfortable around each other. K stares at a wall seeing himself in the basement along with the crossed-eyed people. *It will never go away,* he thought. *Never.*

Katlyn thought to herself as she watched K staring off the distance. One thing Katlyn was still getting used to was K's abnormal behavior. As far as she was concerned, this guy was weird as hell. But even so, she still had no trouble breaking the ice and their communication was getting better between each other. Something Amy would be proud of.

Pausing for a moment not wanting to disturb him from whatever he was doing. "Hey, you there." she called out.

K responded back with a nod. Times would be this when he responded back, but other times he wouldn't respond at all. It seemed almost like he was in another place, so her question was justified, just to make sure he was listening in the first place.

"So you now call yourself K. What does that mean? Is there a reason?" she said.

K gave her a paper, it was a drawing from when he was young and it had the I. At the back it said "Kan" or "Kan't".

"So whether you can achieve something, is that it?" she said.

K responded with a nod. Katlyn of course knew that he misspelled it but she figured this came from when he was young and as a result of no schooling with Amy being his only source of education but still impressive considering his circumstances, at least.

In the past two months, it had been rough and they constantly encountered Zefron's delegates from day to day. It always left them in a bloody mess and narrowly escaping them. Katlyn knew she made the right choice and although she felt she messed up, it is different now. This time, they were resisting.

She handed the paper back to him. Katlyn did have spare cash and over the two weeks she bought some dvds and a laptop.

"You know I was into that too. Those types of philosophical poems. I remember one of my favorites."

"There once was an old man, close to death with a broken body; a life lived with no show of token. He was in pain, worse than a fox that had been maimed, with all these odds against him: age, death, and sickness. He had no business challenging them.

Withered by time and hardship his body was beaten, his spirit however wouldn't stop feeding. The odds made him look small, but with a closer look it made the old man stand tall. Excitement grew as his time was almost due. As he faced what was deemed his final fate, he smiled for he figured it out long before it was too late.

They could break everything like a small stick but the man refused and gave in, for one day he would be just too thick."

K stared at her for a moment before returning his gaze to the wall. Katlyn smiled at him as she plugged in the laptop, turned it on and put on a western movie. As Katlyn opened some food collected over the past month, K's eyes were glued to the television. Seeing how these outlaws behaved gave K a similar rebellious feeling inside of him. He wanted to prove himself. As Katlyn put down the food, K's mind was made up. He would have to beat the I and claim command of his own mind once more.

Later that night when Katlyn was asleep and Amy of course, was with her still in a coma. K sat in his room, entering deeper into his mind. He then found himself in the hall, where the 'I' lurks.

K walked the hall with great fear, looking down, knowing inevitably what he would see. As he continued down, a figure stared him down. Always the tallest and biggest man on the scene, white as a ghost with black boots and black pants but no shirt, jacked like a strongman. He smiled at him.

It was the 'I' himself, the Ideal man.

"So, you came to challenge me, huh. fuckboy?" the 'I' said.

K said nothing in return.

"Well, let me tell you something. 'First of all," the 'I' said walking closer to K. "You know, that fight that you lost? Everyone in that crowd, everyone watching on whatever device, says you threw that fight."

"Almost like you weren't even trying." he said, "Now, tell me was it really because I chose to or was it really you. Think for just a moment now."

"You wanted to be someone so bad. Someone that you could never become, so you created me. The I, the Ideal man. Someone who could do what he wanted, when he wanted, and nobody could stop him. Always the biggest and baddest guy on the spot, that's me." the 'I' gestured to himself, hand to his chest.

"But," he said. "Something happened, you wanted it back, all the pain and misery along with agony. Just like that man that made you his bitch said. You like this shit. Which brings me to now, right here. The ideal man, the version of you that's perfect as you see it. I'm you and you're me. When you want to slaughter something you bring me, a different version of you, in."

"With that being said, when you get the shit beat out of ya. I get the shit beat outta me, when you get fucked, I get fucked. This should all start coming together now, right?"

"The only difference is that when I actually try to fight back, it's definite. I'm going to win. On the other hand when you try to fight back, sooner or later, you're just gonna get punked out again."

"The reason why I don't fight back, because I enjoy it. Relentless masochism." he explained. "Of course if you know I enjoy it, then you also enjoy it," The 'I' said. "And so it comes full circle."

"So now that you made this trip, it would seem that I need to put you in your place." The 'I' said. "Go on, take a shot and make it count." he said, gesturing for K to come forward.

K then ran for him and punched as hard as could, his punch landed on the I's face. The I's response was blank, as if he didn't hit him. Next moment, K found himself on the ground, unable to move with all his bones shattered to dust, his skull formed back. His body shaping his head back to it's normal self.

"What you know, I know." the 'I' said. "That happened instantly, forming back your head was my will and not yours." he continued.

"You're so much of a bitch that you can't even stand up to yourself. You are without any control of your own consciousness, such a pitiful scene it is."

The 'I' pounded him into nothing but meat and formed the meat into a ball and then smashed it. Seeing the meat on his hands, he laughed out loud and said. "That's all you are to everyone. Whether be it a sex toy, or a punching bag. In the end you are just meat used for others satisfaction."

K found himself formed back to normal, standing in front of the I. K felt it, he was holding back a great deal. It was like he said, he was just a toy. The 'I' wasn't even taking this seriously, this was as if it was just a game to him.

The 'I' grabbed K by the head. K struggled to get free but it was no use. The 'I' punched K in the gut repeatedly. As K started to cough up blood, the 'I' kept going. K felt the I's fist in his back now and then eventually, he punched a hole straight through K's stomach all the way through his back.

The 'I' could make himself as strong as he wanted or in this case as weak as he wanted just to make sure that K's suffering would be a long one. K knew this because The 'I' knew this.

K lay helpless on the ground looking up at The I. He saw him come closer. The 'I' then stepped on both his arm and leg. "Remember K, in the end you're still a bitch and you always will be."

K then awoke to find his entire bed soaked in blood, along with his body that had wounds that were coming and going. K lay back in bed, thinking about what The 'I' said. *Always will be, huh.* he thought. His mind then turned into distraught. For once, he thought again about Amy. *I can't let this be,* he thought.

K then thought hard about what The 'I' had said. Just a different version of himself. *That means The 'I' and me are one and the same,* he thought. *A different version of me though, a suppressed self.*

I have to both embrace and gain control of myself to beat The 'I', K thought. K felt his arms and legs crack back into place as he collapsed out of bed. *Embrace the pain,* he thought. *There's been plenty of it already and a lot more to go.*

He felt every bit of it, as The 'I' said, if he enjoys it then that should be the same with me, K thought. Standing on his feet he tries to make it to the bathroom where he would have privacy. He falls forward but catches himself on the bathroom counter.

He felt himself breathing harder, as if choking on something. He tried to gasp for oxygen but none came. He saw himself in the mirror. He was turning blue, his eyes getting ready to pop out. He then saw in the mirror that The 'I' was choking him.

Eventually, he disappeared and the choking stopped, leaving bruises on his neck as a reminder of him. K then regained his composure and tried to steady his thoughts. He could see himself being brutalized constantly feeling this unbearable growing hardship that just wouldn't cease.

He went to his bed and grabbed a picture that he drew inspired from the movie. He watched a movie about the cowboys. How free they were and how they did what they wanted despite their opposition. These men lived in chaos and did things by their own will.

K grew angry at the drawing of this man. He knew there was only one way to be truly free; to have that power to take down anyone and everyone that stood in front of him. To become that figure that would be feared, to be The 'I'; he had to beat the 'I'.

He felt the scars on his neck again, he began to grow furious. Once again he entered his mind once more to go one on one with The 'I'.

The 'I' stood at the other end of his hall waiting for him to come. K began running towards him. As the 'I' waved his hand, K completely disintegrated by the sheer shock wave that came from the motion of the I's hand.

As K formed back he saw the 'I' standing over him. The 'I' then started to stomp on him until he was nothing but meat again and once again, K formed back and tried to continue the fight.

The 'I' grinned as he poked a hole in K's forehead with his finger. And with just his finger, he lifted K up. He then started to tear off pieces of his body, starting with his fingers. Joint by joint he took his time, from toes to torso. He was like a little kid with an insect. Dissecting him piece by piece until only his head remained.

He looked straight into his eyes and said, "Waste is something you always will be. You're nothing more than that." The 'I' then threw the head against the wall. The head exploded on contact creating a giant smear on the wall.

As his head formed back K's pain now has unbelievably spiked. An agony on another level. K however, continued to embrace the pain. The 'I' began laughing now as K stood back up to continue the fight against him.

As K began walking back towards him, the feeling of misery grew with every passing second. K's embracement was turning into something else.

The 'I' backhanded him, sending him back against the wall shattering several of his bones. *He weakened himself again,* K thought. *Only to extend the process.*

The 'I' stared at K as if studying him, like he was watching a movie and his favorite part was coming up.

K now was feeling something else that came from embracing this pain; a suppressed feeling that warped his mind. It was now that he lusted for this growing pain. He craved more of this hardship that was unlike any other, he wanted to feel this growing agony that just wouldn't stop.

"Well," The 'I' said. "Finally, you were able to do it. To access me and become The 'I'. Now wake up and see just how much of a glutton you are for this shit, huh."

There was a knock at the door, Katlyn looked through the window and saw there were more of them: the delegates from Zefron.

As K woke up, he felt like he was not himself. His mind was different, his mood changed. He was now acting as The 'I'. He saw himself in the basement like he always did, being severely brutalized.

"Oh, man. I'm a fuckin ho for this shit." he said.

He felt the pain and how fast it grew. *Ah man, I'm so ungrateful for it it's just not enough,* he thought as he spiked it at will, making it spike higher and faster now. *Still not enough,* he thought. He then heard Katlyn's voice cry out as the delegates broke down the door.

"'Bout time they show up. Giving them the ability to sense me wasn't enough. Looks like next time I'll also have to use the K factor to make them appear. Let the slaughter fest begin." K said.

"A match of will's first." he said. *Huh weak spirit, they already gave up.*

K walked through the door and saw them all. They were holding Katlyn and more were coming towards him. Slowly they filled the entire room.

K then moved, hoping over all of them in the room. He tapped each one on the forehead, before returning to the same spot he entered the room in. It happened so fast, the delegates didn't even know what had happened.

They all exploded covering the entire room in crimson. Katlyn in shock only stood, glued to place, not knowing what had happened. She then looked at the person who was supposed to be K but felt as if she was looking at someone else entirely different.

The 'I' smiled which in itself was horrifying to look at. The eyes that were wide alert as if pumped on adrenaline and his demeanor that seemed uneasy, his mood shifted to a different nature.

K then began laughing hysterically. "Fuck man! I do love slaughter."

He walked around scanning the mess he made, he walked towards the path to a door where Amy lay.

As he approached Amy, K then remembered the time when he was still a young boy. He remembered the cage fighting, how he made the deal with The 'I'. It was all a lie, in truth he never really did go on any winning streaks but he just continued to lose, and that he had taken those brutal beatings.

Even when he lost the fight, backstage they would hold him down and The 'I' would let them take turns on him again. He was never really winning anything.

K looked at his hands, he was just being persuaded by The 'I' again. Even though now that he and The 'I' are one. He knew that as much as he loved to beat others, he loved it so much more to have the beating he was giving to himself.

It's like an addiction that couldn't be controlled, he thought. *After all, this power is being manipulated by a part I suppressed. Letting it out, I've become lost in it. Personality being warped to be someone I've always dreamed to be.*

Someone who does as he wants, when he wants and not one is able to stand against. Power and strength that not one can stand against. But...

He thought back to that night when he killed the head. How he was not in control of himself. This force was not his own; he must make it that way. He struggled and struggled, mind breaking, body being torn.

K now was in the Hall of the I again. This time was different however, The 'I' approached him and stared at him. "You're done here, K. You're fighting against yourself, which is me right? You think that in fighting me again, you will find some other clue that you've been looking for huh?"

"Well that is true but not for this. You see, K," he said as he sat back on his throne. "You're always gonna have to contend with me. This power is yours to earn, but it's mine to control. I fight to hurt others as you fight to hurt yourself."

"That's why I'm here. Moments like this. As long as you resist you'll always be in control of yourself, your actions, and this power you have." he explained.

"Don't worry. I'll be somewhere in a place I created by mind, slaughtering others, while you keep to your own business. But the second you totally give in, you will have to face me again to test yourself once more. Starting the whole ordeal of regaining yourself like you did before to gain this power."

K then closed and opened his eyes. He felt this power; it was absolute. The pain was still growing and the mind was constantly being attacked. The basement, the omni pain, the constant struggle to remain one's self. It was all overwhelming but K remained intact, mindset different, it was now a choice to be this way.

He reveled in the experience now. Choosing pain, somehow fed him in a way, but it never satisfied him. And he wanted more.

Katlyn looked at K who now seemed himself again. She was still stunned at what happened and could not wrap her head around at what had just occurred.

"K." she called as she approached him slowly.

K then looked back at her and saw her frightened, shaking as she walked. She was covered in blood from head to toe. K could see it in her eyes, how she was trying to keep it together as she came closer to him.

On the verge of a breakdown, but somehow being stable. K went to his knees and found himself embracing Katlyn.

He glanced back at Amy and saw that she looked so peacefully asleep. How she slept, he could wake her up right now at his own will. *It would now be so easy just to wipe all these troubles away,* he thought.

But he could not bring himself to do it. This "trouble" was what made him as he is now. His pride and selfishness held him from doing so but Amy wouldn't be in peace with all that's happening now.

K wiped the bloody mess away from the room, making it appear as if it never happened. He was conflicted with himself, this pride that burdened him and this woman that troubled him. He went to Zefron's place which was situated in a basement. Zefron who was pleasantly jovial at K's arrival, only grinned at the sight of him.

K wrote on a wall and then left the basement where Zefron still stood, shaking with anticipation as he read the writing in blood. *Ten days for a torture chamber, something that he wanted to do as promised,* Zefron thought.

This would prove quite the test for his patience. *But why torture yourself like this,* he thought. *I could have some excitement in other ways.*

"Oh the fun hasn't even started yet" he said.

5

Scary things have happened, Katlyn thought. *Scary things have happened. This has taken over my mind.*

"K is something else entirely now." she says to herself as she stares at him. He's lost in his thoughts again, as if in a completely different place.

Another delegate entered the door and Katlyn reacted to the noise. It's only been a day and they're coming in hordes. All the delegates were parked outside the house, as if waiting for something to happen or any signal. The delegate crept into the house and Katlyn quickly stabbed his head repeatedly.

When he was no longer moving, she grabbed his body and tossed it in a room along with all the other dead delegates.

Thirty seven, she counted.

Don't they all have guns? If they wanted to they could all just storm in and completely overwhelm me, she thought.

News must've spread about K. *They are probably aware of it now, thanks to Zefron,* she thought as she had a flashback to that moment when K seemed "different".

Someone then threw something into the house, one glance at it and Katlyn quickly dashed to another room. The front part of the house blew up creating a huge opening. She could now see the delegates and they could see her.

Only one came charging forward. She charged at him with a knife but he caught it. He took the knife away from her. He toyed with her, faking as if he was going to stab her.

"You've been running around a lot lately." the delegate said.

Two more came in from outside and rushed towards Katlyn. They pinned her against the wall, one of them then pulled out some nails and a hammer.

Another woman then went and stared at her. "Yeah, you're pretty fast on your feet." she said while pulling out some nails.

She then steadied a nail right on her feet and hammered one in. Katlyn let out a short scream and struggled but the delegates continued to hold her down. One nail after another, the pain was excruciating, but eventually they finished.

Katlyn whimpered at the stinging pain in her feet. One then took the hammer and swung it with the claw end, hitting her leg. Pulling it out, chunks went with it, her skin was now hanging off of her leg. They all took turns swinging the hammer at her.

Katlyn's legs then gave way and she collapsed to the floor. The nails however pulled at her feet making sure she stayed in place. As Katlyn posted her hand, trying at least to sit up but a delegate with a knife stabbed her hand down on the floor.

Now she was unable to move it. As she motioned for it with the other hand, another hit it with the hammer.

"Won't be going anywhere now." one of them said.

Katlyn's hand hurt, but she could still move it. Slowly she crept her hand towards the knife and made sure it wasn't noticeable.

"Nice place she got here. Wouldn't mind crashing here for a bit after we're done with ya." another said while looking around.

Then grabbing the knife, she stabbed one of the delegates in the leg nearby, causing them to fall with the hammer. She instinctively grabbed it before another delegate kicked her in the face.

They all rushed and tended to the delegate to make sure he was okay. She used the hammer to take out the nails that pinned her feet to the ground. One delegate saw her and rushed to her. Katlyn however hit her with the hammer, making that delegate go to the floor as well. Just then she saw a pistol on her and grabbed it. The two others ran to her and she shot them both dead.

Katlyn then shot the other two that were still moving on the floor. Now, finally she could breathe. Grabbing the hammer again, she pulled the nails out and could finally move. She however is unable to stand and so she pulled herself on a chair and sat on it.

It wasn't until after just a couple of seconds of heavy breathing that she realized something very troubling. The giant hole in the house was big enough for a good sized crowd to walk through. A crowd was staring at her too.

All the delegates were just standing there looking at her but not moving. Katlyn then looked towards K and saw that he was still completely lost in thought. Right now, Katlyn felt as if she was alone in this.

What kind of game is this, she thought.

It's been an hour now and they haven't even moved an inch towards her. She tried to stay awake, but her eyelids were getting heavier by the second. Soon, she couldn't keep them open and as they fell closing completely shut, she instantly opened them to see herself being held down.

As the delegates stormed in, she saw them carrying an unconscious Amy. They pulled out a knife and started decapitating her. Katlyn screamed in horror, and opened her eyes again.

Soaked in her own sweat, she found herself breathing heavily with tears falling from her eyes. Just then she felt her wrists and ankles, and saw marks where they were holding her down.

Then she looked up slowly moving her head and saw all the delegates smiling. Then she saw the blood trail from the outside leading into the backroom behind her. The tears turned into streams. as she now knew the reality of what happened.

She let out a dreadful scream. Madness took over Katlyn and she stormed the crowd of delegates with a knife and hammer. Bludgeoning three to death and stabbing two before she herself was overwhelmed.

They beat her till her face was so swollen that she couldn't see. Katlyn then thought to herself as she lay on the ground just to get beaten so much that her eyes were only closed for a second. She just blinked but that one second was all they needed.

They could've easily have done this before but they were just toying with me, she thought as she heard her pulse growing silent. They tossed her in the backseat of a car and the driver drove off. Katlyn however, still conscious, saw the driver and bit a piece of his neck off instinctively. Unlocking the door, she threw him out.

Now taking control of the car, she began to run over every single delegate she saw. More groups kept coming and she ran them over too. One hour they were still running, two hours. Groups here and there. Third hour, the windshield was constantly being wiped of blood as if it were raining. Fourth hour, she was driving to search out any lone striders she might've missed.

She then saw no more groups, but kept driving to make sure. When she knew that there were no more coming for sure, she went out of the truck and into the house. On her way to the house, she saw a shotgun with shells on a dead body and then she took it. She grabbed a match and started a fire that surrounded the house.

The fire spread everywhere except surprisingly towards the house. Hearing nothing but the roaring flames, she followed the trail of blood to Amy and saw that her neck was bleeding but still her head was still attached.

Not only that but she was still breathing. Katlyn gasped and then sighed with relief. She stared at Amy laying in the bed so peacefully. *Maybe it would be best if she stayed like this,* Katlyn had thought to herself.

Katlyn pulled up a chair and stared out at the doorway with the shotgun and waited to shoot if anyone appeared. Staring straight at the doorway, without sleeping, eating, or blinking for the next nine days.

K finally stood up walking through the walls to see Amy still unconscious and Katlyn still guarding her. K placed one hand on her shoulder and she jumped at his touch but the next second she was eventually fast asleep.

He placed a blanket over her and walked out of the house. A wolf then came towards the house, but it mysteriously turned the other way completely avoiding the house. It was the same with anything else that came by, may it be human, animal, or anything coming turned the opposite way.

The house would remain completely undisturbed.

K continued with one step just outside the house and the very next being right in front of Zefron.

Zefron laughed at the sight of him clearly by how ridiculous he's turned out to be.

Zefron then directed him to his chamber and shut the door behind him.

"Now let it commence." he stated.

6

Zefron was there with him smiling with that sadistic look in his eyes. He put K in chains that hung him vertically in the air. Zefron then pulled out a knife and cut off all his clothes leaving him completely naked. Zefron placed a TV right in front of K so he could see as well what was happening to him.

There was a thin metal pole; Zefron put it into K's anus and kept pushing it forward, maneuvering it ever so slightly. K felt the cold metal inside of him; it punctured his insides and eventually made its way to his penis.

With the thin pole at his penis now, he felt a slight push. He could see the tip of the pole in his shaft. K then heard a cranking sound and looked at the tv. Zefron had a crank and K could see his penis opening up. The thin pole now was like tentacles that kept the penis opened, showing a visible, bloody hole in the shaft now.

Zefron then came in front of him with tweezers and started to pull something out from the shaft. K felt tweezers inside him, he also felt the constant tear of his penis. It was stretched so tightly, it felt like it would tear his piss slit open and it did, only slowly though.

It was very bloody, Zefron wiped away the blood constantly to see what he was doing. K noticed Zefron's intense breathing and heavy sweating; he was enjoying every single second of it.

K felt something move inside of him, and he felt it being pulled out from him with Zefron's tweezers. It was far too big to fit through the penis, but Zefron kept pulling anyway, so the inevitable happened.

It tore open, with his large intestine coming from his groin area. Zefron kept pulling and pulling, eventually stopping once he saw the end of the large intestine. Next he picked up a small knife and made a deep long cut going down from his chest to his split open groin.

Peeling back the skin and muscle, exposing the guts and organs inside of him. Zefron then went to his mouth and stuck a thin metal rod in K's mouth. K vomited in response. As Zefron continued, he stared at K's stomach and watched how it contracted. Zefron only stopped until K stopped vomiting. Nothing would come up now, he'd just hurl.

Proceeding forward, Zefron then cut out all his organs, with the exception of his stomach, and placed them in a plastic bag right beside him. He then started going to work on the rest of his skin, peeling it off, exposing muscle. He put something on K's head and it messed with his mouth. With a remote, he made it move in a chewing sensation.

He grabbed the organs from the bag and put it into his mouth and he chewed away at all the organs in the bag. By this point there was a giant opening from his mouth to his anus, so the chewed organs would just go straight down and spill into the container just below him.

Zefron grabbed this container and spilled it over K. Next he used a special tool to strip the muscle from his bones, extracting all the muscle except at the head and neck portion. Putting the muscle in the same container, he lit them on fire and put it right under K.

Quickly, he grabbed some of the chewed organs and forced it down K's throat and eventually spilled it into the fire which spiked it higher, burning K himself. As K was being burned, Zefron took the machine from his head. Now with a special knife he sawed K's head open and pulled out his brain along with his eyes.

Zefron held it as the rest of K's body burned, and he ate K's brain. It spewed blood with every bite he took.

Zefron exited the room and watched the cameras rolling, recording everything. The camera was watching him as well. Something was going on with his stomach. It started burning, then he knew that he would see K again, and it would be very soon.

His stomach burst open with red mush coming from it. It was the chewed brain, half digested. It made its way to the room where the rest of K was, and he started to form back. K took a step forward, and then he was back inside the house with Katlyn and Amy.

K stared at Amy and Katlyn who were both out for a while now. He finally was capable now of creating something. He could create something now. Something that could act as a reset for both Amy and Katlyn.

K was still seeing himself in that basement and also in another dark place being attacked, tortured and eaten by monsters and hideous creatures that caused him great agony and suffering. He was experiencing all that at the same time; the basement and the dark place, right now as he stood there.

This wasn't hell at all. It was something that was on an entirely different level. Something that made hell look like heaven. This gave him something, suffering that never ceased. This gave him pain that would always grow so fast, and it would always grow faster.

Locking away his power of all knowing, he saw a movie that Katlyn had watched with him, a movie about old cowboys. The cover showed a man with his hat and another old man behind him. Just then something clicked in the boy's mind and he started aging rapidly at will. Then formed a cowboy, hat in his hand.

He then lifted his hand towards Amy and saw her face, how beautiful she looked. K wanted to reset everything but his mind became transfixed on Amy. He wanted to see her smiling face. The surprise on her face would be something to make him joyful again and he would regain that same comfort he did way back then. He made himself believe that at least.

And so he woke her up and slowly she opened her eyes to him, trying to focus as her blurred vision slowly became clear. At the sight of him, she let out a scream that shook the boy so hard, he heard his bones rattle. Amy then stumbled out of the bed to the other side of the room.

She then fell down and saw Katlyn, but with her head dropped low, not showing her face. Decades old now and covered in wounds. She might as well had been a dead stranger to her, Amy couldn't recognize her, at least not in a panicked state.

Amy took the shotgun Katlyn had in her hands and aimed it at K. Amy looked around and said "Where is he? Where's my boy?"

No response.

"Where's my boy?!" she shouted.

K didn't respond; he only came forward trying to comfort her. He was so stunned, he was unable to speak, he tried but just couldn't.

Amy responded with a gunshot. It left three huge holes stretching across his abdomen, but K kept moving forward to her. Amy tripped backward and crawled away into the hallway to get away from him. She could see that he was coming to her fast and with urgency. She ran away from him, heading outside where it was littered in dead bodies.

She could hear his footsteps grow louder, so she ran for the field. Amy should have been able to figure out that he was her boy. In the very least considering that and maybe, K thought to himself that this was a mistake, he should put her to sleep and start over now but a part of him thought that this could still be resolved without the use of his abilities. He was capable of at least making that happen.

Amy then bolted for a vehicle she first saw.

As she twisted the keys to start the truck, Amy didn't notice him but K watched her and this time he moved very slowly as he approached. Desperately trying not to spook her again. He couldn't believe the level of terror in her eyes as she saw him. She didn't recognize him at all. He needed to make her understand but he wanted to do it naturally, without tampering with anything.

He saw her look around the vehicle trying to start it but falling at the same time. The engine must've somehow been damaged. He remembered that face, that face on the night the head was killed; how she was wandering throughout the forest trying to find her boy.

And here he was again with her, putting her through heartbreak once again. This familiar feeling of incompetence started to overwhelm him but he pushed to stay focused.

Amy grew ever more frustrated and punched the window out to release her anger. Her hand started to bleed profusely.

I haven't lost him, I haven't lost him, she kept saying to herself.

She tried to start it again and this time it was successful. Then as soon as she looked up, it was as if a cold shiver rushed through her entire body. With the air escaping her a moment, she forgot how to breathe.

This man was right in front of the car. Amy ran him over, quickly regaining herself and backed the truck up running him over again. She then sped away leaving him in his broken, crushed and mangled state.

Amy drove back, driving through the hole in the house, crashing her way inside, only then remembering to step on the brakes. Getting out of the car shaking as if she was about to have a panic attack right there, she ran for him. In the room there she stopped, finally able to think for a moment and upon closer speculation looked at the woman who was still unconscious.

"Katlyn" she said out loud. She knew she wasn't dead from the breathing she felt from her.

Looking at Katlyn however, she noticed how she was a bit older. Amy looked at herself as she was older too, but she would question this later as she was still paranoid that the monster would still return.

No, she thought. *I ran him over twice. There's no way anybody could survive that.* She picked Katlyn up and carried her to the truck. Amy tried to piece it together, she had to be asleep for some time then. But if that was the case, then wouldn't that mean she would have trouble moving now, after being immobile for that long?

She got in and put Katlyn inside then climbed in the driver's seat. She switched gears and drove out of the house. But then, the engine failed. Amy calmed her nerves before they started to go array. There was no reason to hurry, that monster was down and she had gotten Katlyn; now was a time to take a breather.

Just then the image of him shot through her, he was still moving forward.

"No." she said, trying to stay rational.

He was splattered on the ground, completely crushed. He should be gone.

She looked outside a window and saw nothing but dead bodies. *What on earth happened here?* she thought. Before she left the house, she made sure to check everywhere for him all the while she carried Katlyn into each room. But he was not there.

That monster she saw he had to have known, she thought. She drove back and saw that he was not there. Then she felt someone breathing right beside the broken window of the car. Amy shook horribly as she slowly leaned over and unlocked the passenger seat getting out that way. She grabbed Katlyn and went towards the front of the vehicle. Her eyes started to water and burned.

The monster she saw began to follow them but Amy kept walking away from the truck and eventually she stopped. This monster had something to do with her boy going missing, something to do with Katlyn being the way she was now. Her blood began to boil.

She lifted the shotgun and fired a shot at him. This monster fell backward, but had gotten up. Another shot was fired, once again falling backward with his hat coming off flowing in the wind. *One shell left,* she thought as she looked at the chamber.

"Where is he?" she shouted, fighting back tears.

The monster didn't speak but only moved forward. She fired the final shot, not at the monster but at the vehicle directly behind him. An explosion happened as a result. It swallowed the house and the field surrounding it. Amy searched for the monster, but she couldn't see it anymore. But yet through furious flames, she felt it stare right back at her.

She lifted Katlyn and continued forward through the flaming fields. She thought nothing about the flaming fields and being cautious around them, or if she would make it out without dying in this fire, but thought only of the boy she lost. However, she kept moving forward, with eyes streaming with tears.

K was on fire, engulfed in the flames, stared out with one good eye as he watched Amy marching through the fields seemingly without care. He took in everything, from his hat swimming in the wind, to the grass blackened by the fire, to Amy's tears washing the field at her feet. As K's hat rode the wind, he thought this would be an appropriate time for the reset and so it was.

Ronnie

The old man sat on a couch looking up staring off at his clock. In the other room, he hears the deep sighs of his beloved wife as she's fast asleep. *It's true what they say, your life really does flash before your eyes, at least in my case anyway,* he thought.

He's looking at the hands of the clock, but he saw something totally different. He's caught in a trance and now he's somewhere else.

He's a lot younger and found himself with a paintbrush. He's almost done with the picture and now he's deep into his creation, until the alarm went off. This startled him; he caught himself before he spilled his paint. He lets out a sigh of relief.

Six thirty, it said on the timer. Ronnie knew it would be cutting it close. He had promised his wife that he would cut his time in his studies short, all in an effort to spend more time with his wife. Although sacrificing some of his time in his work wasn't something he was excited for at first, over time he eventually became accustomed to it.

After all, being busy with the kids all day and along with work getting in the way, morning was really the only time available for them to be alone together.

As he walked down the stairs towards his room. He realized he was drenched in sweat. *Ugh, I smell terrible,* he said to himself.

He opened the door and upon entering the room, he saw his wife. She was wearing one of his shirts while she lay in the bed watching TV.

"The caveman reemerges from his dormant state. How's the painting coming along?" she said.

"It's going." he answered back.

He had been married to Serena for a couple of years now. Although those had been happy years, Ronnie began to take notice of her demeanor. He knew that to avoid another "incident", he had to tread lightly.

Although Serena was taking some of his personal time away, she could not be blamed for wanting to spend a little more quality time with her husband; it was a just action to be taken.

However, it also could be argued that over the years, Ronnie had become increasingly more uncomfortable around Serena and that he could not be blamed for either.

He entered the bathroom to turn on the shower. He picked out his clothes while the shower was turning warm. Finished with choosing clothes, he finally entered the shower.

As he stood in the shower, the water felt so nice that he could fall asleep, then he remembered how Serena had taken a picture of him, when he decided to doze off in the bathtub. She even sent the picture to everyone he knew.

Everyone laughed at the sight of him. But if he was to be honest, it was just as embarrassing as it was funny.

That however had passed, and now served as nothing but motivation not to do it again. Exiting the shower and drying himself, he finally put his clothes on and stepped out of the bathroom. The bedroom was silent, and Serena was gone.

"Hmm not even giving me a chance this morning." he said.

Shouldn't have cut the conversation short about the paintings, but she knows I can't talk about it. It's my own private work, he thought to himself.

Wait a second. I'm jumping the gun, he thought. *She's just gone to get an early start on making breakfast. Yeah, that's it.*

He walked downstairs and saw her actually preparing food in the kitchen. The sight relieved him; he was right. *All is well,* he thought.

Just then footsteps were being heard from upstairs.

Two kids came down, Damien: his son, and Teresa: his daughter.

"You two are up early today. What's the occasion?" Ronnie asked.

They both froze looking confused and surprised that their father was here for breakfast in the morning.

"We're going over to our friend's house." Damien said awkwardly.

Ronnie was perplexed especially since Serena didn't run this over by him the other day.

"Hurry up and get your bags. Your food has already been placed inside." Serena said.

There was a knock on the door and both Damien and Teresa scurried away, with a familiar face shutting the door behind them.

"You didn't want to let me know that both our kids were going to be away for the day." Ronnie asked rhetorically.

"Just came up, sweetie. Thought it be best anyway, for them to mingle with their friends outside of school." Serena answered.

"Anyway," she said, changing the subject. "I noticed that you've been spending more time in your studies lately. Is there anything big?" she asked.

"Well, nothing other than what I'm doing." Ronnie said.

"You don't want to talk about your work. It must be big with all that time you're spending in there. It's almost like you're not even here anymore." she persisted.

Ronnie knew where this was headed; he had to be very careful and choose his next words wisely, but he was also growing frustrated with these questions she was asking him of his work. She knew it was his private hobby and that he did not like talking about it.

"You have the morning with me Serena, I thought that was the deal." Ronnie remarked

"Well, you've been cutting that pretty close, so close to where it's been non-existent. That and the kids haven't seen you in two days. Every time you walk around, they look at you like a stranger." she said with her voice showing anger.

Ronnie did have to admit that it was the truth. He had been cutting it close in the mornings and he'd be an idiot if he didn't notice how detached he's been lately. However, being so into his work now, at this point in his project; he just couldn't sacrifice anymore time away.

"Yes, I do see that but with the project almost being done, I just can't step away from it now. The sooner I get done with it, the better." Ronnie countered.

"That wasn't the case with the last one." she said, gripping the plate harder in her hand.

Ronnie was seeing the signs clear as day. He was walking on a very thin line now but at the same time he was growing impatient by this conversation. This was his escape from her and she was trying to take that away.

"I'm sorry but…"

Before Ronnie could even finish his sentence, a glass plate was smashed against his forehead. He fell from his chair to the ground and instinctively held his head. His wife, Serena stood in shock of what she'd just done.

Ronnie saw this coming from a mile away, yet he didn't care, not until now anyway. He was irritated by the constant thought that his work overcame his relations with his family. But now he questioned if it was really worth fighting if this would happen.

Ronnie stumbled to the bathroom, leaving a trail of blood. There was a deep cut on his forehead, just above his eyebrow. He washed the wound thoroughly, applied alcohol and held his hand there while he searched for something to cover it.

He put some large band-aids over it. He carefully put them over the wound and pressed down gently. He stared into the mirror to see if it would stay. In just a few seconds the band-aid came loose and the cut opened and was exposed again.

Ronnie let out a heavy sigh and applied more adhesive bandages. He then walked to the living room and sat there on the large couch. With one hand up holding his head while he stared at the ground.

"Sweetness." he heard but he didn't lift his head up, he knew it was Serena. "Here's your breakfast." she said as she placed the plate in his lap and took a seat right beside him.

The food was hot, like it had just been cooked.

Ronnie stared at the food without moving.

"Well, aren't you going to take a bite?" she asked.

Ronnie then started to eat only looking at his plate trying not to look up at her.

After eating some of the eggs he worked his way up to her eyes. They were staring right back at him with a smile.

As Ronnie stared back, he saw all of her details, red hair, hazel eyes; a small and petite woman, very beautiful. Yet it was a frightening sight that froze him stiff. He thought about how welcoming her demeanor was now and how this made things all the more scary.

She began to raise her hand and Ronnie's eyes fell back to his plate. She started rubbing his forehead, gently touching the band-aids over his wound.

"Want to watch a movie?" she said.

Ronnie cleared his throat nervously and said, "Um. Yes, what?"

Serena turned on the TV and scrolled through the channels looking for something to watch.

"Do you have any preferences?" she asked.

"No, none." he said.

Serena then turned to a comedy show and put it on to watch. She leaned and rested her head against him.

"Sweetness." she said. "I'm sorry for what happened earlier. I just wanted us to have a happy time together. I guess I just overreacted."

"Of course." he said in response.

"You know it's good having you to just myself again, just the both of us alone." she continued.

"Yeah, it is nice." he said in agreement.

Serena then rubbed her hand towards his groin but Ronnie grabbed her hand, caressing while slowly moving it away.

Serena on the outside was calm, but on the inside she was furious. She however, couldn't really be angry with him especially over what just happened in the kitchen. She decided to persist a little more and kissed his shoulder.

"Um Serena, I think I'm a little sleepy now. I think I'll be headed to bed." Ronnie said as he got up.

"Sure, you've been up all night" she said in an agreeable tone.

It wasn't until he closed the door to the bedroom, that she started crying. Ronnie heard her crying her eyes out while he was upstairs. He loved his wife deeply, but he had to stop her, that was a little too much of a turnaround from the kitchen.

Serena eventually pulled herself together and phoned a close friend that she knew. She heard the phone pick up on the other end.

"Hello." a man said, on the other end.

"Drake." she said. "How have things been with you?"

Drake had been a longtime friend of hers and former lover as well. They both confided in each other, Serena telling secrets to him that she couldn't even tell to Ronnie.

"Yeah, everything is fine over here. How about you?" he said. "You don't sound too good."

"Drake, it's Ronnie. Things aren't working out so well now. I just don't know what to do." she said. "I can't even keep him in the same room as me."

"What happened, Serena?" he said.

"I happened." she said. "It gets so frustrating." She sighed deeply, trying not to cry again.

"Hey, if he's still around that must mean something, right?" Drake said, trying to comfort her.

"I don't know." she said doubtfully.

"If you don't know, it might be best to find out." he said.

"Find out?" she said. Just then her mind started to flutter and she had an idea.

Serena knew she would have to find out if Ronnie really loved her, but that was a lie she only told herself. This would be something for her own amusement, in response to how her own husband just acted.

She told Drake about it, and Drake didn't have any qualms with her idea. Serena went upstairs to Ronnie and closed the door behind her.

"Ronnie." she said. "Please forgive me."

Drake did not live far from the house and so the drive wouldn't take long at all. Serena climbed into the bed and on top of Ronnie.

She knew that this wasn't the way Ronnie preferred it, but he would do it if she forced him to.

"Serena, I'm not really in the mood right now." he said, trying to push her off.

She grabbed his hand and said, "Why don't you stop being weak and act like a real fucking man?"

Ronnie stopped resisting, as Serena kissed his face and rubbed his groin.

"Just you and me, sweetness." she said. She rolled over, making him become the one on top.

"Love me." she said. And just as she said, he started loving her.

She grabbed his face and made sure his eyes were on her. The car pulled up and Drake stepped out. He went inside, unlocking the door with a spare key given to him by Serena herself.

He went in, headed straight upstairs and saw Ronnie who was now being intimate with his wife. Drake took off his clothes and approached the bed silently with Serena watching him.

Drake then quickly pinned Ronnie down onto the bed with Serena still under him, smiling in his face.

"What." he said as he tried to turn, but he couldn't as Drake held him down.

Drake then started loving him from behind, Ronnie still tried to resist but it was no use as he just wasn't as strong as him. Serena slapped Ronnie and told him to fuck her, and so he did as she said.

Serena laughed and got out from under him, sat on the side of the bed and watched with great satisfaction.

"You're nothing but fuckmeat in this room with me, boy." Drake said, as he started fucking him harder.

Drake put his hand around Ronnie's throat and started choking him.

"Look at me." he said. Ronnie stared into his eyes and Drake came.

"Wow, your wife really was right. You are a weak man." he said.

A few moments later, Drake fucked his wife right in front of him, and he fucked her hard. Serena screamed his name and Drake came on her smiling face and the rest on her husband's face.

Drake then left with Serena shortly after she cleaned herself. Leaving Ronnie there alone in his humiliation and degradation.

Now leaving his trance, he's back to his chair. *Ah yes, I remember that and the next day that came. How the house was so empty and that no one showed up*, he thought. However, he also remembered how strongly he wanted to redeem himself.

This desire was what led to him taking a combative class. He showed up at the front door and saw people inside actually fighting. The sight of it intimidated him, however at the same time this proved how real this was, if sparring was allowed.

He went and saw people just standing around conversing on various topics. Together they sounded like indistinct jumbles. Comparing himself to the others, some looked out of shape and others looked in peak physical condition. He himself wasn't too much of a weakling at first glance.

In contrast, he certainly wasn't a picture of an ideal star athlete either. Someone then called the class to form a circle. During the first half of the class, they drilled certain moves. Ronnie stuck out like a sore thumb not knowing the terminology or how to properly do the move.

They laughed and smiled at him. This agitated him greatly. It reminded him of the humiliation that had just happened. He looked like a joke and a weakling. The same weakling that Drake did what he wanted to do to him.

Then it was time for sparring. Still trying to clear his mind, he put on protective gear to shield his head and waited until it was his time on the mat to go. It didn't take long for him to get taken to the ground. The man on top started raining down punches on him. The fight was then stopped and they moved on to the next pair.

The protective gear did well, but not well enough, his eye was swollen and his cheek was bleeding a little. As he watched the others spar, he took off his head gear. Now he could only think of the guy on top hitting him repeatedly and how everything was so easy for him to do.

A guy came up to him and patted him on the shoulder. "Hey, man. I didn't realize you were new. Sorry 'bout that." he said.

"Oh no, it's fine." Ronnie said in response.

"My name is Peter by the way." he said.

"My name's Ronnie."

"Listen, if ever you need someone to give you extra help, I'm here for ya." Peter said.

"Thanks, I might have to, after that." Ronnie said, shaking his hand.

The class finally ended and Ronnie exited the gym.

As Ronnie walked to his car, Serena saw him with his bruised face. She wanted to go and talk to him to make sure he was alright but knew that it wouldn't be the best choice, at least not now. His expression looked somewhat disappointed, most likely in himself.

As Ronnie got into his car and drove away, he constantly thought of the man still punching him. He got to his house, shut the door, went upstairs and lay on his bed. The kids were still gone, his wife still away with someone else, ever since that incident in the kitchen and honestly Ronnie couldn't care less. Right now, the house was quiet and all he wanted to do was sleep.

As Ronnie slept, he dreamed of Drake and how he handled him any way he wanted. That didn't sit well with him. He awoke in sweat and as if instinctively, he headed towards his study room to paint.

Once he sat on the chair, he did not leave until he passed out. This time it was a pleasant sleep. Upon awakening, he found himself on the floor with half of his face covered in paint.

"Must've spilled." he said to himself.

As he looked at his painting, he realized how shocking it looked to him.

This was mostly however due to the fact that he had completely forgotten what he was doing in the first place. A man whose body was breaking like glass, this man was trying to pick the fallen pieces of himself. Trying to put himself together as he was falling apart.

Ronnie began feeling dizzy and so he quickly exited the room, collapsing in the hallway. He tried to stand but found that he couldn't, without falling over again. He decided to sit back against the wall until whatever it was, had passed.

He heard his pulse race and he could feel his head pounding. His eyes started watering and couldn't keep his eyes open. They would have an unbearable sting to them if he kept them open.

He heard a door unlock and he could hear a voice. It was Serena, she walked upon him in his tragic state and she phoned an ambulance for him. She tried to talk him down but it seemed to only make him worse.

All she could do was try to hold him and wait. Eventually the ambulance came and they escorted him to the emergency room.

With Serena being told to wait outside, she was scared as to what happened to him, wondering what caused this to happen. A doctor then stepped out to see her. Serena stood up to her feet at the sight of him.

"Seems to be a case of severe stress, coming to him all at once." he said. "You don't know what may have led to this happening, do you?"

Serena paused for a moment, because she knew the answer was so obvious that it was funny.

"No, just stress from work maybe? or normal family matters." she answered back.

"Well, now he needs a lot of rest so you can talk to him but only for a little while." he said.

Serena was escorted to his room and once Ronnie saw her his heart rate rose significantly. They took her out of the room and told her it would be best if she returned next week.

2

_____

Ronnie was drifting in and out of consciousness, he didn't even know where he was half the time now. Then he saw Serena's face, and that made him have a bit of mixed feelings.

Now he's back on the chair. Funny how he remembered being in that hospital bed so vividly. Ah, yes his wife, he wondered back to when they were kids. Though he remembered how it wasn't a pleasant being around her, even in those times.

He found himself in the house of the girl of his dreams. He was just in middle school, but he was sure that he found his soulmate. He looked up and saw that she was gesturing at him to come into her room.

It took a lot of tact to trick her parents into thinking that Ronnie had left early and it was even more of a hassle to keep him hidden all day until both of her parents had gone to bed.

Ronnie ran up the stairs and went into Serena's room. Once he was in, he was frozen by what he saw, Serena had a black eye; she tried to cover it up upon seeing the expression on Ronnie's face.

Ronnie still did not move a muscle all he could say was, "Serena."

"Don't worry, Ronnie. It'll pass." she said.

But that was the problem, he thought. The reason he was frozen stiff wasn't because she had a black eye; it was because she had this for the third time in the past two months.

"Why does he keep doing this to you?" he said nervously.

"Don't know, just being my dad." she said as her face started turning red.

Ronnie also noticed that every time he mentioned her dad, she would get into a fit. He knew Serena hated her father and how detached he was from her unless he wanted to give someone a beating.

"Serena, maybe you should let someone know about this." he said.

"No." she said firmly. "I want to do this myself." she said.

Ronnie knew how badly Serena wanted to kill her own father and how scary it was to be around her at times. Sometimes she would specifically describe how she wanted to do it.

Ronnie looked at her and wondered if her hatred for her father was one of the things making her sick, both mentally and physically.

Her mother was led out on an errand, so she would be gone all night. This was the perfect night to act on it, and Serena intended to do just that.

"Serena, maybe there can be other options than that right now." Ronnie said.

"Ronnie, this had to be done." she said.

Although Ronnie was admittedly scared, he sadly had to be honest with himself. He did admire this side of Serena. How she had to do something by her own means rather than somebody else doing it "their" way. He wondered though, if this was too far.

Serena gave him a long piece of wire. She noticed Ronnie was shaking a little when she gave him the wire.

"Ronnie, you can do this. Don't worry." she said.

Ronnie nodded in agreement and they both headed downstairs to where her father was sleeping.

Ronnie felt his heart beating faster as they opened the door to his room. Sure enough he was there, sleeping like a baby. Ronnie wanted to back out now but knew that it was maybe too late.

Ronnie felt his breathing grow even heavier by the second. Serena placed her hand on his shoulder in comfort. Ronnie was to approach him first; he would be strangling him and holding him in place, while Serena had the knife in her hand ready to stab him.

Ronnie was in position ready to do it. Serena was staring right at him while her father was asleep. Everything was weighing on Ronnie; he was the deciding factor and so he acted.

As soon as Ronnie had the wire around his neck, Serena started stabbing at him mercilessly; she was like an animal. Each time she stabbed she would drag the knife down, making blood ooze from his stomach.

Ronnie held the wire at his throat as he struggled ferociously. He saw the blood trickle from his neck as a result from the wire cutting through the flesh. Her father struggled and kicked Serena away. Ronnie tightened his grip around his neck and more blood came from him.

Serena immediately got back up and continued stabbing and racking the knife across his body. He then stopped moving and fell over, but Ronnie still had the wire against his throat. As he continued to fall with him, his head came off.

When he hit the floor, his stomach twitched and his intestines fell out through the wounds he received from Serena. Ronnie could only stare at the mess he participated in, a headless and gutted corpse; he was part of this now.

"Whoa, nice work, Ronnie." Serena said, with so much excitement. "You got his whole head to come off. Looks like you might be stronger than you look." she said while squeezing his bicep.

Ronnie looked at Serena but didn't smile. "Serena I..." He stopped in mid-sentence out of shock.

"Listen, Ronnie." she said. "This wouldn't look good if I were to be the only one left unharmed in this scene."

"What…what are you saying?" Ronnie said.

"Ronnie, I want you to take this knife and cut me with it." Serena answered.

"Serena, I don't know if I…."

"Yes, you can, Ronnie." she interrupted him.

Ronnie took the knife and raised it to stab her, he slowly moved and froze.

"Here, let me help you." she said.

She put her hand on top of his and guided the blade into her arm, she shuddered at the pain. Next she made him do a few slashes at her chest and stomach.

"There, that should do it." she said.

She grabbed a t-shirt and wrapped it around her arm where it was stabbed, the cut was deep but the t-shirt was tight so it should hold it.

"Ronnie, thanks for the help. Leave, before someone finds you." she said as she grabbed the knife and wired rope. "Hey, take these and put them away in a trash can on a street along the way back to your house."

Ronnie grabbed them and left. As he ran, he heard, "Thanks again."

On his way back to his house, tears started to form from his eyes. He tried to hold himself together until he got to his neighborhood. He threw the wire and knife in a nearby dumpster and went straight to his house where his parents were still asleep.

He put the clothes in a bag and put on new ones; he then threw those clothes away too.

The next day he heard that there were police at Serena's house last night. They found no leads and as the story went, Serena survived an attack from a break in and that her father was killed.

As time went by, the case went cold and remained unsolved. Ronnie still went to see Serena and they both became very close; however, Serena met a guy named Drake and they were together going into high school.

With Drake going far off for college and Serena going elsewhere for her education they both split, leaving Ronnie with Serena by the end of high school and marrying her not too long after.

Although still keeping in touch with Drake, Serena would become close friends with him and their relationship becoming even closer than her and Ronnie.

It's a joke how things can be so obvious. There right in front of your face, the whole time and yet you pay no attention to it at all. At least not until you're a victim of it, yet even still, you try to ignore the problem.

A monster that's staring back at you all the while it's eating you alive. And as you stare back at it, you just close your eyes and pretend you are somewhere else. When it's over, you act as if the blood isn't there. That your arm isn't torn and that right now, the same monster isn't chewing on it being content until the next time it gets to strike back.

You soon begin to speculate things, seeing what you did wrong this time or maybe you should have tried a different approach other than the one you took. Acting as if it was your fault that any of it happened in the first place.

In the end, the monster does as it pleases regardless of how cautious you are and if it decides that it wants another arm, leg, or head; it will have its will.

Ronnie then brought himself back to the first days of marriage with Serena. They were bittersweet to say the least, but when those times were pleasant, it definitely made up for the times that got ugly.

The day had started off so well, remembering the smile that only she could do. How the day was quiet and relaxing and then a debate started on what to eat for the night. At this point, Serena's heart problem had gotten worse and with her responding severely to her medication, she needed to watch what she ate, especially products high in caffeine.

Dinner was already prepared with a movie that Serena missed in the theatres ready. Serena wanted to watch it that night. However, she knew that staying up this late would be a challenge for her and that some coffee might do the trick; Ronnie, however, didn't think it was so hot.

"Serena, I'm sorry. But I can't let you touch this, at least not tonight." he said.

"Ronnie, you have to be kidding me." she stated angrily. "This our first date night together and you won't let me have this."

"I'm sorry Serena but we'll have other times too. This won't be the only time." Ronnie reassured her.

She knew that he was trying to help her but she was growing more frustrated not by the caffeine but by something Ronnie couldn't help.

Serena was reminded of her father at times and how he controlled her. This led her to not taking directions very well. And with Ronnie being a man, it only reminded her more of her father as well. A father that took everything from her, neglecting her and a constant reminder accompanied with beatings that he controlled everything, but her.

She had to show Ronnie who was in control. That was the first time Ronnie saw that look in her eyes, how it was almost like instinct. She took out a knife and stabbed his hand down to a counter, pinning it there, and leaving him unable to move.

"Who in the fuck do you think you are? Trying to enforce something on me?!" she yelled. Then her face turned to horror at what she had done.

"I'm sorry, I'm sorry." she repeated over and over.

Ronnie was at a complete loss at what just happened. Serena quickly bandaged him up with one of her shirts and ran water over the wound. Since then, they always kept a first aid kit around the house. That was their first incident together, just on the second day of their marriage.

Ronnie would find out more about the horror that made Serena more of a plague to herself as she was to others around her.

Ronnie carefully walked around the bedroom being as quiet as possible for Serena not to wake up. Yet as he turned around, there was Serena staring right back at him suspiciously. Her expression then turned to worry as she continued to stare him down.

Ronnie eventually broke the growing awkward silence in the room "Is there something wrong, Serena?" he asked.

"Ronnie, won't you lie down for a moment? There is something I have to tell you." she responded.

Ronnie did as she said and went back into the bed.

"This is about your father?" Ronnie questioned.

Yes, it is." Serena answered.

"I'm sorry for what I did last night, sweetness." she said with sympathy. "It's al..."

"No, it's not Ronnie." she said, interrupting him. "Ronnie, please believe me. I can't control that part of me. It's like there's a different person there."

"You see, Ronnie. You saw me with a black eye, but that's only when I was allowed to be seen with others." she said as her voice cracked.

"He would beat me so severely to the point where I needed to be hospitalized. He wouldn't let me eat for weeks if I disobeyed him, not even letting me go to the bathroom." she said with her voice breaking.

Ronnie found all this hard to believe but in the end, he chose to believe it. He had to, after all it was the reason that he justified himself for killing her father in the first place.

"I'm not telling you this for you to feel sorry for me but I'm just telling you so that you get the reason behind it. I know that what we acted in wasn't what you wanted and I know it bothers you sometimes, but in the end, we did the right thing."

She put her hand on his cheek and kissed him. Ronnie did believe that they did the right thing, but at times, it felt like maybe he shouldn't have been there at all. Ronnie decided to stay in bed, but Serena went to the bathroom and stared in the mirror.

She looked and saw herself but what was she really? She had scars from her childhood that could not be forgotten. What she did to Ronnie was completely out of line. She instantly regretted it the moment it happened. She asked herself if it was right to tell some of the things her father had done to her. Of course, it was, he had to know, but what did Ronnie think of her now?

The anger she felt every time she thought of that man, it was suffocating her. It was an unbearable feeling that she couldn't shake off. As a consequence of it, her actions are almost impulsive. She was sweating now. She had to keep herself together or it might happen again.

She hated feeling like this; she hated who she was. She hated what she saw in the mirror. Why did she have to be this way? Her eyes became red with strain. Finally, she blacked out.

Ronnie had heard a loud thud in the bathroom. He immediately got up and yelled for Serena, but no response came back. He ran and found her on the floor, he called her name as he picked her up and she woke up.

He laid her back in bed and saw her staring at him. They both stared and finally they both kissed.

Of course, through those years of being together and not just being married, Ronnie began to think as he lay in that hospital bed. Did Serena really think of him as a weak man? Someone incapable of standing his ground?

He always knew himself to be the passive type, but was forgiving her really something truly the right thing to do? How she was able to have an incident and then she was able to carry on after an apologetic speech. Even Drake said it himself, he was a weak man.

He felt like a fool, only until now that he had started loathing himself even more. Once it hit him that this was a repeat offense. He sacrificed for her because he loved her deeply, he loved her so much that he was willing to endure her madness.

She was with him because she wanted someone to control, someone to have power over, all this stemmed from her father and Ronnie was the perfect candidate of choice. No one better to fit the role. Time after time, Serena was able to have her way with him whether to have someone as a punching bag or someone to humiliate.

Now Serena was with Drake who was her former lover. This was definitely a terrible joke, but in the end still a funny one. It was very funny to Ronnie now.

Now, he knew himself to be less of a man than he originally thought himself out to be before. Now he had exposed himself.

Ronnie still went to the combative class and was excelling in it, but still now he came home to whatever remained of his former life. A wife that was no longer there and kids he doubted would ever return.

This sight made him one angry man that constantly thought of how to get back at everyone. This anger was then used as motivation, a driving point to introduce something as a last ditch effort when he became too desperate; it was clear that he was not in his right mind.

The old man sits in his chair, waiting for this moment when someone would come knocking on his door. Of course, he knew it would not be death. Why? He faced him every night and he'll know the face of death the moment he sees it.

Death would be quite a sight for the old man to see. He looked forward to it, seeing what horror it had to offer. Once, it showed him his worse. He would challenge it as he laughed in its face. *Oh, that would be glorious,* he thought.

A woman then wheeled him to an empty room with a table. The old man stared across from the table and saw that it was his son.

"Well, if it isn't Ronnie." he said. "So, has it been 3 years now." the old man said.

"No, it's been about a week now." he said. "Remember, today is the day that you get out and come home."

The man had just gotten out of the retirement home and now was going to spend time with his son. Though, he was close to death now with a terminal illness that affected his memory and made him hallucinate from time to time. So, Ronnie could only speculate on how long that would be.

"Ah, yes. Right. Now, I remember." the man said.

Ronnie then signed a few papers and took his father to wheel him out. Ronnie wanted to ask his dad at least something to break the silence, but he knew all he did. Day in and day out was just him staring at that clock, all damn day.

"So, what reason are you bringing me out here, boy?" he asked.

"Well, I just wanted to spend time with my old man." Ronnie responded back.

"How's the family?" he asked, getting straight to the point.

"My wife left me," Ronnie paused, then continued. "and the kids are gone. I don't know where they are either."

The old man looked at Ronnie and a smile slowly grew over his face as he continued to stare at him.

"Please." the old man said. "Take me through how it all happened, boy. Then, I can show you how to fix this problem."

3

___

Ronnie had to admit as much as his dad had unsettled him, he knew that he was his only choice now. With his whole world gone, his father was the only one he could turn to. His dad went to write out his plans on a sketch in the other room.

Ronnie sat in another room taking in what he had just done. His father was a man not to be entertained; he knew this before heading forward with asking for his help. His father was a loving father but only in way of first hand experience, could anyone understand or even comprehend.

His father, Christopher Holman, had a list; it was a bucket list of things to do before death. This list had made him not a well-liked man among many. He valued himself differently than other people might.

He eventually would complete his list, but only to add more into it. A wide range of actions, be a force to be feared.It's what he started out as, murder and genocide. Having one of the worst reputations at the time, he carved a man's face into a frown. With just a letter of how happy this man was, until he met him.

The party house incident: No one knew how it happened, but his father had somehow put a combustive element in the drink, and once everyone made a toast, it detonated. It wasn't some fiery explosion. His father had apparently tested out this substance and had modified the combustion to the point where it let off a small explosion, just light enough to where you could see the insides fly out.

The guests wallowed in pain and you couldn't see any burns at all, just red blood and guts that flooded the floor.

Following this incident, Holman was prosecuted but with a good lawyer, had gotten off somehow. One night in his house, Serena was sleeping over and Ronnie, were both watching a movie on cowboys. His father had come barging into his room and threw open the bathroom then closed the door. He grabbed Ronnie and put both him and Serena in one of the bathrooms that they had and told them to lock the door.

Men had barged in, and Ronnie heard every action they did onto him. The beating, the cracking of bone, the rape as he groaned. Ronnie could only stare back at Serena, and she stared back at him in horror. He could hear his father begging for more. He fell to his knees as he heard more profanities being thrown around as they continued ganging up on his father.

And with heavy breathing they left the house.

"Come out now, son" He heard from him.

Ronnie jumped back at the sight of him. He was horrifying to look at. He asked him what his father was thinking.

He replied, "I was thinking that these guys might go all the way and kill me."

"Why did this happen?" Ronnie asked, demanding an answer.

"The power of will." he said, nonchalantly "Just something else to check off the bucket list."

Of course, Ronnie hadn't understood it then, nor does he understand it now but he wondered but dreaded to ask. Did he still have more to cross out on that list?

"Hey, son" his father said with a raised voice. "Soon. I think it might be a good time to call your mother."

"Really?" Ronnie said in response.

"Not now, but soon." his father said again as if never hearing Ronnie.

Ronnie had hated his mother, the lack of love she had for him. The no-care attitude, this was what led to her leaving the family, and Ronnie hated that.

Of course, their relationship had a rocky start when his mother and he were still in middle school. Dating someone like this man at the time. He did wonder, what was she up to now.

"Hey, son." Holman said. "It's time for our first trick."

After just texting Serena they both sat at the table, waiting on the phone to vibrate, signaling a new message.

"How do you know that she'll respond so soon?" Ronnie asked.

"Your wife is still into you. She probably regrets doing what she did. Doing this will cue her to come back and make amends to you." Holman responded.

"Sometimes it's hard for me to see that. Especially when she loses control like that." Ronnie said.

Holman put his hand on Ronnie's shoulder. Just then the phone vibrated.

Ronnie read the text. "Alright, she's coming over."

"Remember to go for the neck once she turns her back, to go to the far room." Holman instructed.

Ronnie nodded in agreement.

Moments later, a knock on the door came. *Wow that was fast,* Ronnie thought as he ran to the door excitedly. He then stopped and realized this was the woman that had abused him for years. Now, she's back and he rushed to her. He had to recompose himself now and handle the situation. He peeped through the door and sure enough, it was her.

As he opened the door, the sight of her elated him and he embraced her as she embraced him. She held his face and said how sorry she was for what she had done. Ronnie knew she was, but his father was right about something. He had to assert himself with her or else she would only do more damage to him, if that was even possible now.

"Go put your stuff in that room over there." he said.

She did as he asked without any complaint. As soon as she turned her back, he got her with a syringe. She let out a painful groan before falling in Ronnie's arms. Holman then came wheeling himself in the room

"Get her phone." Holman said.

Ronnie then took her phone and froze for a moment.

"What's the matter?" Holman asked.

"I can't get through her phone." he said sternly.

Holman then held his hand out and Ronnie passed the phone to him. Holman was perplexed by what he saw.

"Dots on a screen." he said. "What's this?"

Ronnie had guessed the pattern and unlocked the phone for him and Holman went through her calls and messages. *Turns out she has a close friend who she's been hanging with,* Holman thought. Although he already knew this, it was all clear now.

Now, staring at the woman, he struggled not to grin.

"Alright, Ronnie tie her up." he ordered. *This is going to be glorious,* he thought to himself.

Serena awoke in a stupor with her blurred vision focusing on an image. Eventually her eyes focused and the blurred, shapeless image formed into Ronnie, who seemed to be in distress.

"Ronnie." she said while trying to regain herself. "What's going on?"

Serena tried to move but found that she was tied to a chair by rope.

Ronnie hesitated but finally spoke. "Serena, I can't just let you off this time."

"You have to pay for what you have done." he responded as he rose from the chair. "But I can't bring myself to do it."

"Because I know that when you get mad, you don't see me." he stared right into her eyes. "Instead, you see someone else totally different. So, I got someone who will find another way to make you see."

"No. Ronnie, I'm going to help make you see." Holman said as he motioned for someone else to enter the room. It was Drake.

Ronnie was perplexed by this, but before he could even open his mouth, Drake slugged him one in the jaw, making Ronnie fall backward to the ground. The sudden shock of what Drake had done stunned Serena.

"Drake, what the fuck are you doing?" she cried.

"Now, this should be really interesting." Holman said, as he looked at the camera that peered into the room.

This was all like a fun spectacle to him, like watching a movie and his eyes were glued to the action.

Ronnie struggled, appearing to be dazed by the punch he just took. Drake then grabbed him and pinned him against the wall, choking him. Just when Ronnie was about to black out, Drake would let go and choke him again to just let go at the last minute. This was like he was controlling him. Showing him that he had control over him. Like he was a god.

Drake then held a half-conscious Ronnie to the wall and started punching him in the gut. He would wind up his punch slowly, as if to deliberately show Ronnie that it was coming. Ronnie's arm twitched from the muscles cramping from the lack of oxygen getting to them. He couldn't even defend against it.

Each time the punch connected to his stomach, he let out a sound as if he was about to hurl. He could barely regain his breath before the next punch came.

Shortly enough, blood started hurling from his mouth but Drake kept going.

"Explain." Holman said over the small megaphone that echoed into the room.

Drake let go of Ronnie as he was holding him by the throat.

Ronnie fell down to his knees, throwing up the lunch he had earlier today. Drake then made eye contact with Serena and walked to her. His look was full of fear and regret.

"The fuck is wrong with you?" she said to him.

"Serena, a bomb is strapped to your chair." he said.

"What?" Serena responded.

"If I don't do what Holman says, then he'll blow this whole room up and electrocute me with this neck brace I have on." he said, pointing to the thing on his neck.

"Holman." she said.

This was worse than she thought. Holman just disappeared from her and Ronnie's life. It was assumed that he was killed or locked up somewhere, but now he's back and apparently with more games to play.

"Why is he doing this?" she asked demandingly.

"He wouldn't say. He said all would fall into place as this situation unfolds. That was just what he kept repeating. Over and over until I walked in here." he said.

"Attack!" the megaphone spoke.

"I'm sorry." he said as he turned his back on Serena and faced Ronnie again.

Although it seemed Drake was forced into this situation, he enjoyed beating down on Ronnie and would've done this with no coersion. But the collar on his neck was just a precaution by Holman. Drake would have to deal with him after this.

Ronnie hated this, a lot more than he felt he should. Once again being the weakling, once again at the mercy of another who did as they wanted. Ronnie tried to pick himself up and he was succeeding until Drake smacked him down to the ground again.

Serena thought to herself that if Drake did stop, then Ronnie would be blown up along with her as well. This couldn't end well. Nevertheless, she neither believed that Drake was truly sorry. He had always hated Ronnie and she could see it, plain as day as he tried to hide his grin while he pummeled him.

Drake held Ronnie by the throat. "C'mon, is this really all you can muster up to do? This isn't even a fight." he said.

Ronnie's blood boiled with every comment that came from this man's mouth.

"Give me a shot, right here." Drake dared him.

Ronnie tried to lift his arm for a punch but it only dangled and twitched from the effort he gave.

"Oh, that's right. Punching bags don't hit back do they?"

Ronnie then had a reaction; he spat blood in his face as soon as he said that. Drake's face then turned to anger and he slammed him down and savagely beat him. Ronnie then lay on the floor unable to move.

Holman looked at Ronnie to make sure that the adrenaline shot he gave him was working so there was no way that he could pass out. Added to the fact that he also gave another drug to make sure that the shot wouldn't numb his nerves. It was important that Serena would see the pain in Ronnie's eyes while this happened.

Ronnie however, saw his wife's eyes. How they desperately yelled at them "I'm sorry." but he also couldn't stand it. At the same time how it almost pitied him as well. He felt himself crying and the tears went down. He couldn't stop them from coming down his face.

"Speak." Holman said to Drake.

Drake then walked towards Serena again who was on the verge of crying upon seeing the sight of her husband.

"I'm sorry." he said again.

"No, you're not." Serena said before Drake could even finish his sentence. "I see you smiling every time you fucking hit him. You're lying, right in my goddamn face."

Drake began to laugh and without saying a word, he only smiled at her. Suddenly there was a buzz in her ear. She flinched a little from it but regained composure.

Just then Drake was ordered to give her a shot of sedative. The effects were to be immediate and Drake was told to untie her then exit the room.

Drake then pulled out a needle and said "Don't move." as he injected the shot into her neck.

In just a couple of seconds Serena went limp and Drake instantly began to untie her.

As soon as she was freed from the rope, she shot up from the seat and grabbed it. Then she ferociously started beating Drake with the chair as hard as she could. Drake was now unconscious and on the ground in a pool of blood. Parts of him looked broken but Serena raised the chair again.

But just before she could hit him again, she was shocked and went unconscious. Just before she blacked out, a wire was running through her arm, an electric wire.

Just before Holman told Drake to sedate and get Serena out of the room, he told Serena that the sedative would be faked, but Drake wouldn't know that. He also told Ronnie that it would be faked as well and to see Serena's reaction.

"Now for the next phase." he said as he wheeled himself out of the camera room to set up the next scene.

Ronnie woke up with himself back in the same room. He now could feel sores and bruises that made his body ache from the beating that Drake had given him. He was still shaking. He stood up to see that Serena was handcuffed to the wall.

He realized that she was having trouble breathing and that she was choking. He ran to her on instinct. As soon as he moved, pain shot through his body. The beating that he took definitely left him in bad shape but still stubborn as ever to get to his wife. He endured through the pain.

As soon as he touched her, there was a buzz in his ear, it was Holman.

"Can you hear me, son?" he inquired.

"Dad, why are you doing this?" he demanded.

"I'm doing this to fix the problem that you told me of, son. Don't you want to know how to stop your own beloved from choking?" he said.

"What is there to do?" Ronnie responded in a panic.

"Hit her." Holman said flatly.

Ronnie was stunned by the response but one look at his wife's face turning blue and he couldn't linger in asking another question.

As he motioned in for a punch, his father said, "Make sure that it's a hard one, if you want it to stop."

Ronnie then hooked her in the face. Her face started to light up and return to normal, she was actually breathing a little more easily. *But that was the problem,* Ronnie thought, *she shouldn't be having trouble breathing at all.*

"What's going on?" he asked.

Holman then buzzed in again. "It's a repetitious effort." he said. "It has to be consecutive and over a certain period of time and she'll be breathing normally again."

"Wait!" Ronnie yelled for him but there was no response.

He saw Serena's face turning blue again. Ronnie not having a choice now, realized the reality before him. Serena, although barely conscious could make out what was happening before her. She nodded her head at Ronnie signaling a "yes" meaning that she was okay with it.

Ronnie clenched his fist and with tears, started wailing away at her. He closed his eyes but he could feel his fist connect with her face. It was horrendous. He stopped and opened his eyes and could hear that she was breathing but she now had a blackened eye, her face became swollen purple and bleeding in several parts.

He looked away from the sight but she was still having a little trouble breathing. *Just one more punch should do it,* he thought as he raised his fist. But before he was about to lay down the final hit, he felt a tug at his shoulder. It was Drake again and he was in shock, in utter disbelief at what he was seeing but at the same time, his face showed anger above it all.

"What in the fuck do you think you're doing?" he said as he punched Ronnie sending him to the ground.

He grabbed Ronnie, picking him up from the floor and threw him across the room. Drake then turned back to Serena who began choking again.

Drake looked at her, he put his arms on her shoulders as he went to his knees to see what was happening. Ronnie then got up and hit him at the back of the head. This had stunned Drake for a moment. He stood up and backhanded Ronnie away.

Serena continued to desperately grasp for air, but she was already on the verge of passing.

"Drake, you don't get it." Ronnie said, trying to stand up again.

"Tell me then. What's going on.?" he persisted, wanting answers to his questions.

"Hitting her will save her life!" Ronnie yelled.

He looked past Drake to her and saw she was trying to get air. Ronnie ran past him. He didn't have the time to convince him, especially when he can just show it to him. This time with no hesitation he punched her hard, but there was no response she was still choking.

"How?" Ronnie yelled.

There was a buzzing in both Ronnie's and Drake's ear now. Holman told Ronnie that he had to contend with Drake while trying to save his wife's life. At the same time, he buzzed in and whispered in Drake's ear that the only way to stop her from choking was to kill Ronnie.

Drake had a devilish smile forming across his face, while it seemed like Ronnie was in desperate straights as they both looked at each other from across the room

Ronnie then turned to continue to rain down punches on Serena while Drake had reached for him. Drake picked Ronnie up and slammed him to the ground; kicking him in the face repeatedly. Ronnie, however, had grabbed his foot just before he was about to kick him again. Ronnie stood up and yanked it, making him lose balance and fall.

Ronnie then hopped on top of Drake, pulled his shirt over his head, and started wailing on him ferociously. Then he went to run for Serena and without hesitation started hitting her again. Her face was completely bruised but Ronnie didn't care as long as she stayed alive.

Ronnie, however, felt a tug at the back of his shirt and Drake slugged him at the back of his head. Yanking him away from Serena again, Drake grabbed hold of Ronnie and slammed him down on the ground repeatedly. He turned Ronnie over on his back and stomped on his abdomen.

Blood burst from his mouth, and he could see his vision was going dark. Drake then put one hand over Ronnie's throat and the other hand made a fist and started punching Ronnie. Ronnie's face was now pouring blood from every impact. He could hardly tell what was going on now.

Keeping his arms up, he grabbed Drake's punching arm and bit it. Drake, who was stunned, stood up andRonnie quickly kicked him in the shins, sending Drake to the ground as well.

Ronnie then got up and started to stomp at Drake's head repeatedly until he stopped moving then ran over to Serena and as if instinctively, he continued to punch her, with each hit harder than the last. With his arms burning and knuckles bloodied, his earpiece buzzed.

"Stop." said Holman.

Ronnie collapsed to the ground in exhaustion. He could see Serena drooling blood now.

"A box was at the far corner." Holman buzzed again. "The code is 7482."

Ronnie went to open the box. In the box was a key, he picked it up and freed Serena from the handcuffs and carried her out of the room.

Ronnie went to place Serena down on the couch carefully, then went into the other room where his father was. But as he opened the door and peered inside, he found that Holman was not there.

There was a note on the wall saying. "You'll thank me later."

4

The next day had come and it appeared that Serena's face had swollen significantly. She could barely speak, now that her eyes were swollen shut. She would drift in and out of consciousness. When she was awake, all she could do was grunt.

Ronnie considered calling the police, but he couldn't, especially when the story was that he had done this to her and how his father had made him do it. With the blood from his knuckles and her face intermingled. They would surely find out that it was him.

Courtesy of his father, however, someone was supposed to be coming over to help him. This person was to be trusted and therefore no worries were to be met. There's that and Drake's dead body from downstairs would be disposed of. The cleaning would be done this morning with no trace and no questions asked.

Well, if Holman trusted this person, then he shouldn't need to worry. After all, what choice did he have? He cared for Serena deeply. It was all coming to him now and it hit him hard.

Tears were pouring from his eyes, he was now wailing. *I did this*, he thought as he looked at his own hands. Still bruised and wet from the last time he had washed them. He saw that she was once again unconscious and then the doorbell rang.

That must be the person, Ronnie thought. As he ran to the door and opened it, he saw that it was the last person on earth he wanted to see now; it was his mother.

His mother said nothing as she entered the room, avoiding eye contact. It was only until she stood in the middle of the room that she spoke.

"Where is she?" she asked reluctantly.

A closer look at her now, he could see that she was old late 50s? early 60s? Yet she significantly looked younger than his father. Wearing shorts, black tennis shoes and a loose fitting shirt. She seemed like she was going to be moving a lot today.

"She's in the bedroom. I'll walk you there." Ronnie said, walking past her not wasting a moment.

Soon they both found themselves in the same room as his wife, Serena. His mother sat beside his wife and pulled out a needle. He rose up.

"What's that?" he said defensively.

"It's just a little anesthesia shot to keep her asleep so she can be properly cared for." she answered.

It was quiet in the room as she thoroughly placed the shots in different parts of her face. Ronnie constantly stared at his mother with anger and great curiosity at the same time. His mother in contrast, did not do so much as to even glance in his direction the entire time.

Ronnie grew even angrier by this. Not so much as a word had been said to him. For the first time in a long time, was any interaction made between them and it turned into this. Though, Ronnie was not a one-sided fool. This had to be very uncomfortable for his mother as well. Especially considering that she was the one that left.

Now for some odd reason, she came back. This, however, wouldn't be the place to raise any discussions about it. It would have to be after she is done treating Serena. The room was quiet as it was inevitably growing quite tense. Silence only being interrupted by Ronnie who asked a question for what his mother was doing to Serena.

His mother gave a faint smirk at his questions being asked back to back. It seemed like she was transported back through time where he was still a little boy, asking of every action she was doing. When he saw her doing something that piqued his interest, like something on the computer or with a nearby neighbor that had a minor injury that she had to treat.

Of course, he didn't see the dark side of it. When someone would end up with a fatal wound or when his father would do something stupid, relating to that goddamn list. She found herself shaking. She erased that thought from her mind and continued.

She took a good look at Serena's face and turned her head slightly. Applying some type of substance to the cuts on her head and with a few stitches, she stood up and gave Ronnie some medicine and substances with instructions on each of them to help with the healing process.

She then turned and headed towards the doorway.

"Wait a second." Ronnie said. "I need to ask some questions."

The woman shook her head and said no without looking at him.

"I believe I am in the right to at least ask a few questions." Ronnie said, growing more assertive as his anger became more apparent.

She kept moving towards the door as if he hadn't said anything. He grabs her shoulder, stopping her.

"You're my mother and you can't even sit down for a minute to talk?" he pressed on.

She shrugged his hand off and opened the door.

"Haven't seen you in a while. Don't you just wanna talk for a little bit?" Ronnie asked. "Isabella Holman, right? My father wanted me to talk to you. He was keen on me doing so. Don't you want to stay for at least a little bit?"

"There is nothing more to say between us." she said as she closed the door on her way out.

He stared at the door for a moment. Through an opening between the curtains he could see her walking away.

"Wait, she didn't drive here." he said. He went outside and saw her walking to the direction of the highway.

"Hey!" he yelled out to her. "I'll give you a ride."

But she didn't respond back. He ran out and felt a raindrop. *Weird,* he thought. *It was just sunny a few moments ago.* The sky was now getting dark and cloudy.

He got into his car and started his engine. By the time he looked up, she was halfway across the field. *Man, for an old woman she sure can move,* he thought as he drove through the road where they met. He made sure to drive right beside her.

"Hey, where do you live?" he asked.

Isabela just continued to stare at the road as if he didn't say anything.

"Hey, I can let you sleep at my place, you know. It's not a problem to me, with you helping my wife and all." he offered.

Isabela scowled at the gesture he just made and quickened her pace. Ronnie, however, stepped on his gas a little and still kept beside her.

"Listen, I'm not going to leave this highway unless you get in the car." he said.

The rain changed from drizzling to pouring and it came down hard.

"This is ridiculous. Just get in the car." he said to her.

They soon both entered a single lane leading off to the highway. Soon he heard someone honk his horn behind him. Cars were trying to get past him but Ronnie stood his ground. *There is no way I'm leaving like this,* he thought.

Isabela felt her hands go numb and soon she couldn't feel her toes. She was feeling cold and completely soaked. Ronnie eventually left his car and ran after Isabela. He grabbed her and felt how cold she was. Isabela yanked his hand off, and Ronnie took a step back in shock.

Then before Isabela could react, Ronnie picked her up, threw her in the car and drove off. Once inside the car, Isabela unlocked the door, opened it and attempted to leap out but Ronnie caught her by her shirt and yanked her back in.

"You know, don't you think that you should stop? I mean, at this point,you'd be doing me a favor." Ronnie said.

Isabella thought for a moment and then relaxed herself, eventually falling asleep in his car.

As Ronnie pulled up to his house, he turned to look at her while she was asleep. He stared at her, and saw how pleasant of a sight it was. He leaned back and lingered in this moment before moving. He could really go to sleep right now, but resisted the urge to.

He hesitantly went to tap his mother. *Please don't cause a ruckus,* he muttered to himself. She woke up and saw him gesturing towards the building,motioning for her to get out of the car and into the house. Ronnie gave his mother some towels to dry herself off then gave his mother a bed to sleep in as he always had one guest bedroom ready for any occasion.

He then sat down on the chair, right beside the bed where his wife Serena was sleeping. He folded his arms, leaned back and went to sleep as well.

"Dad, what's the purpose in all of this?" he said to himself.

He awoke at the sight of his wife and to the smell of something cooking in the kitchen. He went down to investigate and saw that it was his mother who just finished making breakfast. She passed a plate to Ronnie, they both sat down and ate. This was a pleasant experience, even though his mother, with the food preparation, made herself at home really quick.

His mother grew more relaxed. Compared to how she was when she was here yesterday. Although she seemed a little agitated this morning for some reason. As they finished up the food, Ronnie only had questions at the forefront of his mind, he had to ask them.

"I want to ask you some questions." he said in a polite manner, trying not to give tension in the slightest.

His mother's eyes stayed on her plate. "Okay." she responded back.

She knew this would eventually come. Now seemed to be an obvious time to do it. She tried to prepare herself, but it didn't matter, she knew she wasn't ready but it might as well happen now.

"Well, I guess I want to know your name first." he said.

"Isabella Cummings." she said.

"Isabella Cummings Holman?" Ronnie questioned.

"Yes." she answered back.

"How'd you meet my father?" he asked again.

Isabella took a deep breath and let it all out. Ronnie saw the tears form in her eyes; she smiled at him gently.

"At my school." she said. "First year in middle school. That's when I first met your father."

Ronnie's face twisted in confusion but his expression changed to shock. He figured it out already, the age difference between them both were all too noticeable.

This, however, should not have hit him as much as it did now, but still he tried to deny it.

"You two were school love birds." Ronnie said.

Isabella shook her head.

"Your father had long since past his school years by the time he saw me." she said, still looking down at her plate.

Ronnie fell silent, trying to absorb all of this in. His mother knew that this was hard for him, as she remained silent, giving her son a moment to accept what he just heard.

"I saw him looking at me once. The way his head turned, following wherever I went. How his eyes were focused so much on me. I never saw him blink. That was the first time I noticed him but I couldn't say that was the first time he noticed me."

And just like, that it seemed as if Isabella was transported back in time, reliving the events as she spoke about them.

"I would see him every day, as I exited the school. He would already be right there waiting for me to come out. He would sometimes be in his car or maybe in a building, but I would always notice him somehow. Other times, however, he would be quite bold. Standing on the other side of the street looking at me."

"It made me slightly uncomfortable, but I knew that he wouldn't just walk up and take me. Especially in a public place such as that. Even more certain with disappearances happening recently around town."

"One day, I had gotten into a fight with my parents. So me, in my simple-minded rebel ways, ran away. It was only until I was far enough from the house that I noticed him staring at me. Just as he did at my school, except this time it wasn't a public place. It was me and him alone in the dead of the night. My spine tingling, feeling nothing but a cold chill and him with his grin turning into a huge smile going from ear to ear."

"He took me by the arm. I tried to pull back, but as soon as he noticed me forcing his grip away, he turned and smiled at me. He waved his finger and shook his head, mouthing 'No, no, no' while having the biggest smile on his face."

"Putting me in his car, we drove off to his place."

5

He motioned Isabella into his bedroom and locked the door behind him. There were two separate beds and he pushed her forward to one.

"Here are your clothes for tomorrow princess" he said as he placed a set of folded clothes near her on a dresser.

"You can go to bed, when you're ready." he said while turning on the television. "Well, here's the remote, in case you want to watch anything else."

A sitcom was playing, Isabella stood there for a moment.

"Go ahead, princess. Get into bed already." he suggested.

"Your legs will get tired standing there like that. You'll surely feel it by tomorrow." he said.

"Why?" Isabella asked him.

She tried to be assertive and firm in how she spoke to him, but she just ended up sounding scared with her voice cracking towards the end.

He said nothing and just put his finger over his lips. "Get some sleep, princess. You've had a long night already."

Isabella went into bed fully clothed, down to her shoes. She had no intention of staying the night there at all. The plan was to wait until he slept, then she would get away. She couldn't sleep even if she wanted to. She rolled over to the side facing away from him.

She stared at the empty wall for God knows how long. The only thing going through her mind was, if that man was looking back at her, smiling the same smile he did earlier tonight.

Isabella didn't know how much time had passed, but it had to have been a while now. She slowly turned back over and saw him, he was sleeping face up. She stared at him for only a moment before mustering up the courage to get out of bed.

She slowly creeped her way towards the door and eventually made it there. It's all said and done now. The moment she opened this door, She could book it downstairs and once she made it to the front door, she would be home free. As she twisted the doorknob, her heart raced but as soon as she pulled the door open, it made an unbearably loud sound.

Isabella turned to check if he was awake, and thought that it was a stupid idea but even then, it didn't matter. He was standing right behind her. There's no way that he could have responded that fast. She would have heard some movement.

Perhaps he wasn't sleeping at all. Silently following her to the door, waiting for her to discover the sound.

"Where are you going?" he asked.

"I wanted to go to the bathroom." she said, lying through her teeth.

He pointed at a bathroom that was on her side of the room. She replied with a thank you. As she went to the restroom, he knew that she was clearly lying. He closed the door and went back to bed.

Isabella stared into the mirror and started crying. Curling into the fetal position, she whimpered to herself. She stayed there for the rest of the night. Upon waking up, she heard some shuffling in the room but she didn't want to go out just yet. She made sure to lock the door behind her when she entered the bathroom last night.

Knowing for a fact that he can't come in there, that gave her some comfort. When there was no more noise, she opened the door. Nobody was there in the room. She sighed in relief at the scene. She saw a note on the pile of clothes that he placed on top of the dresser last night.

It read: "I'll be out for the evening, so make yourself at home. Make sure to clean yourself. The smart TV and remote in the room are yours. Snacks are in the mini refrigerator."

Weight seemed to have been lifted from her shoulders. *He's gone,* she thought. *Oh, he's gone but just for now.* She immediately went for the door and heard that dreadful creaking sound, but that didn't matter since he's not here.

She walked out just to find herself slamming against something hard. She caught herself before she fell backwards and saw that what she hit were metal bars. Grabbing them, she sank down to the floor. She let out a painful groan at the sight of it.

Soon, she found myself breathing erratically, as if she's about to break out wailing any second. She lay down on the floor and turned over staring at the ceiling. She stayed there for God knows how long, but it must have been the whole day because she heard the front door open and close.

Hearing the footsteps come closer and closer to her, she still continued to stare at the ceiling. It didn't matter to her.

"I see you've gotten comfortable." he said as he went past me.

He noticed that she still had not changed into her new clothes nor did she take a shower. He opens the mini fridge and sees that the food had been left untouched.

"I know all of this is new to you, but please give it a shot. After all, you might just like it here." he said.

"I'm afraid, you have to take a shower. Here let me help you." He carried her to the bathroom and placed the clothes that she had to change into.

On his way out, he closed the door behind him and left her there. Isabella sat up and brought her knees to her chest, hugging her legs. She didn't move a single muscle and she sat there for a while, until she heard a knock on the door.

She jumped back at the sound. After a few seconds of silence, she heard his voice.

"Are you alright in there?" he asked

She didn't respond.

A few more seconds of silence, came and went, then she heard him say, "Alright I'm about to come in".

He waited for a few seconds, as if he thought that she was putting on clothes. Waiting for her to give him the signal to come in but she did neither of that.

He slowly opens the door and sees that she hasn't even started taking a shower.

"Oh, you still haven't cleaned up yet, huh?" he said.

He looked around for a moment and eventually found something else to say.

"Ah well, what's one day huh?" he said while putting her clothes back.

He left the door open for her to come out, but she stayed.

"Oh, do I have to carry you everywhere?" he said jokingly, with a smile on his face.

He placed her on top of the bed. He turned her body to a position where she was sitting with her legs dangling off the bed, facing him.

He sat down on his bed and his smile grew wider. It was almost as big as the night he saw her walking away from her house.

"I have to tell you what happened at work today." he said all too enthusiastically.

"So, you don't know this, but I'm a bartender during the night. Just picked it up as a hobby of mine to tie up some loose ends, but anyway, tonight I laid eyes on such a queen." he said dreamily.

"Oh, you should've seen her smooth skin. Her blue eyes were so amazing it could've been mistaken for sapphires. That smile, she could light up the darkest room. My lord, she was a scene. The way she spoke with so much confidence in her voice, reassurance in her tone. And then she finally looked at me from across the bar."

"Her eyes locked dead onto mine. I froze and a chill shot through me. The sensation was so raw,I found myself dropping the glass that I was cleaning with a towel. I was so mesmerized. I lost awareness of where I was and what I was doing.

"Those few seconds, I heard no sounds and saw only her." he said. "Almost like how it is with you." he said while tapping my nose with his finger.

"When I went to get a broom to clean up the broken glass, that chill that I felt was gone. It was now replaced with this heat that kept burning within me with every second. I didn't know if she was still looking at me or not. I decided to look up anyway, and as soon as I poked my head up to look at her, I saw that she was laughing."

"I tried to give her a smile to regain my composure, but this was torture. I had to remove myself from the scene. I went to the backroom and I slammed the door shut. I was able to take a deep breath."

"Princess, let me tell you that with someone like that, I need to have them on my terms. They need to be in my environment. To where I can do to them as I please with no ramifications."

When Isabella heard him say that she shook a little bit. He looked up as if concerned and went to put his hand on her shoulder. She backed away avoiding eye contact.

"I'm sorry, princess. I seemed to have overstepped my boundaries but anyway, I did manage to get out of the bathroom. And after the night at the bar, I did manage to follow her to her house. I even took pictures of her and her car."

"Tomorrow night is definitely going to be something else." he said with too much excitement but this time, with a sinister feel to it.

"You can go to sleep." he said. "I just wanted to tell you about my day." There was an awkward silence for a short while.

"By the way, how was your day?" he asked with great curiosity.

Of course, Isabella didn't respond back to him.

"That sounds uneventful." he said jokingly. "Hey, you and me just might end up getting real close if you'd let me, princess. Welp, goodnight princess." he said as he got up and went downstairs to his bathroom.

That's it, she could wait for him to come back up and then she could jet past him before he closes the door.

She waited intensely for his return. Soon, she heard his footsteps. He was coming back up, he opened the door and she shot past him into what she thought would be the way downstairs, but it ended up being another chained door blocking the stairs.

She stood there in astonishment and she heard his voice again.

"I'm sorry, princess. Really, believe me when I say that. You should understand that I have to trust you first before I can extend your space. I know, it's like I'm holding you like an animal and yes, I am but it has its purpose. Don't worry though, princess. This has some perks and you know what? Since, you're eager to extend your space, I'll do something tomorrow to accommodate that. Okay?"

She got up to her feet and headed for the bed, with him closing the door behind her as she entered. He'll accommodate that, he said. She'd hang on to that, as pathetic as it sounds now. She'd hang on to this psycho's word.

Waking up early the next morning, Isabella saw that he was gone once again. There was a huge paper placed over the doorway with the words written "TA DA!!!"

She went through the doorway. With the door already open, she saw that the way downstairs is still blocked off but there was a door to her right. She saw that it also had stairs leading downward. She went to check and saw that it is another room, which seems completely normal.

It had its own bathroom too. It had a very relaxing feel to it as well. A TV and mini fridge, and a bed for one. It seemed to be the dream room. She finally spotted a paper reading, "It's all yours".

Isabella then lay on the bed. Everything was just so comfortable that she forgot that she was still in the house of a psycho.

It was weird how she still felt a little sleepy though. She then finally took a shower and washed herself since she thought that she was unusually stinky after one day of not taking a shower. She heard his voice calling out to her as she just got out. After putting on some clothes, she went back up the stairs. It was then that she saw him again.

"Dinner's ready once you come up, princess".

Okay, she began to think to herself. *So, he's willing to do things to make me feel comfortable. What I need to do now is to build his trust, then I can escape. I mean that's what this whole thing is about right? Him not completely trusting me.*

She did have a few questions for him, however. Like, how he did he do all this in just one night, without waking her up. I'm pretty sure the way down, which was locked off, was the only possible way to get downstairs.

She walked to the room upstairs where he's holding out her plate for her. She grabbed it and sat down on the bed next to his.

He noticed and said, "You know you don't have to sit up here with me. You can go down to your room and eat too."

"No." Isabella insisted. "I'd rather stay up here and watch something."

He tried to hide a smile as he turned the TV on. *Already making progress,* She thought to herself. They sat and watched the television in silence for a couple of minutes. Eventually, she tried to get him to talk.

"Umm... so about the room downstairs, how long did it take you to finish that?" she asked him.

He choked on his food a little and composed himself. "Yes. Well, it took quite a while but seeing as how uncomfortable you were at first, I decided it was worth the effort. Just a couple of days and nights. Nothing too hard to work through though."

"A couple of days and nights." she said questioningly. "I thought you did it in one whole day. Why was it only yesterday that you said you would accommodate me?"

"Yes. Um, the room has always been there. It was before I met you that I decided to do it." he said, looking down at his food.

"But you said that my discomfort motivated you to go through the days and nights of work to finish it." She said, growing more confused by the conversation.

He started grinning. "Honestly, princess. it was a bit awkward for me to tell you straight out. I thought it'd be best to do it this way, with you figuring it out on your own through conversing with me. So that, I would be forced to tell you."

Just as he finished his sentence, his smile disappeared.

"I don't think it makes it any easier though." he said

Silence grew again and it lingered. He looked out into the hallway avoiding her gaze and said. "I drugged you. You were out for a week now. That gave me the time to work on the room and give you new clothes too."

She was frozen by the response and found that she couldn't move. She was completely speechless.

"I realized that you were growing more anxious and frustrated by your situation. I thought you wouldn't do so well after a week. So, I kept you drugged up until your room was finished."

His eyes worked their way towards her. She forced myself to say some words.

"I understand. I mean, I couldn't imagine waiting another day. Drugging me was probably the best option." she said, lying through her teeth.

"Oh, you do?" he said. "Well, in the end, it was all for you. I'm glad you understand." he said.

Isabella nodded and we both continued watching tv together.

Another two months passed by and she ended up being somewhat comfortable around him. He eventually expanded her living quarters in every part of the house except for the basement. Another six months passed and eventually she still thought about trying to escape. She looked forward to him coming home every day now. It felt like she's so close to winning him over to the point where he could trust her to go out. But after spending long amounts of time away from almost anybody, it did feel nice just to have someone to talk to. Today, however, he brought her down to his basement and stopped in front of the door.

"Hey princess, remember when I told you about that woman that caught my eye a few months back? Would you like to see her?" he said.

A bit confused, she said yes, and he opened the door to his basement.

At first, she could see nothing but darkness. He turned on the lights and she was blinded for a moment. Once her eyes finally adjusted, she could finally see clearly again with the scene that unfolded before her very eyes, all she could do was stare. She ran out of the basement and into her room. She stayed there the whole day until she fell asleep.

She opened my eyes again and saw that it was just a dream. It was morning now, and she got up to see him again. He was in his room. She went and sat next to him. He turned towards her and she saw that his eyes were worn, as if he'd been stressed a lot recently.

"Hey, princess." he said weakly. "Did you sleep well?" he asked.

"Yeah, I did, but I had the craziest dream about this basement area and you were trying to show me this woman you met." she said, almost enthusiastically.

He then covered his face with his hands.

"Princess, that wasn't a dream. I'm afraid that was true."he said silently.

She laughed at him but he wasn't laughing back. So, the image of that woman did not just come from a dream. She was actually there. She stared down at the ground.

"She's......not the only one." he continued.

She had a question to ask him but she was too afraid of what his response would be. So she kept quiet and kept her questions to herself.

"The bar that I run downtown is where I meet some of them. So beautiful and energetic, their charisma is so powerful but I couldn't get the chance to talk to any of them and when I do it's a complete mess. They need to be in my domain." he said.

Suddenly, everything felt so familiar now and she felt that same fear when she first met him. She saw from her peripheral vision that his hands fell to his sides and his head slowly turned towards her. He stares at her and she could only imagine that she looked the same as when she first showed up here. If you could sum it up in one word; scared would be perfect.

"Listen," he said. "I want to be completely honest with you. That's why, I had to show that to you. You don't have to worry about actually going there but I would have to let you know that that's my place to get lost in."

"But sometime today, I would like you to watch some of the things that I do there. I'll be down there in thirty minutes. Please, come with me." he said.

"I might just give you the option to leave." he said.

He got up and went to the kitchen to clean up. She glanced at the clock stuck on the wall and she sat under it until it was time. She went down the basement, the door now right in front of her and saw him standing there waiting for her. At the sight of me he smiled with delight.

He opened the door for her and she asked him what he wanted her to do.

He replied, "Just watch. That's all I want from you, princess."

She went inside with him and saw something hanging from the ceiling. They were little kids, on something that seemed like a conveyor belt. Going around in circles, they spun around like a spinning chandelier. He flicked them to the side to make them spin faster, eyeing his options.

He stepped away and walked towards a cage. It contained a man who's bound on the table with rope. Forcibly making him take the frog stance. There's a metal pole in the cage that he picked up. Isabella tried to look away, but he told her to keep watching. So, to not frustrate him, she did just as he said.

He shoved the metal pole in the anal cavity of the man. He then continued to push it in until it got stuck. The man shrieked in agony, the sound he made was incredibly painful to hear. That's when he took a hammer and hit the other end of the pole hard making the entire pole go deeper into the man's body. With every hit, he screamed louder and louder, until eventually he stopped hitting the man.

The man on the table didn't move an inch, he then motioned her to walk around him. As he reached to see his face, he saw his eyes were glazed over;a sign that he was dead. His teeth all fell out and spread out in front of him. The front of the pole had crashed clean through his mouth.

Everything seemed to be a blur because all she could remember was her being in her bed, looking back at him. She never wanted to go back down there ever again.

Isabella began to realize that everytime he went down there, she wouldn't see him anywhere in the house and the basement door was ajar. It's been days now that he's been going there more often. She hardly ever noticed that he's even here. When she doesn't see him all day, she'd wonder if he's always down there. She tried to escape several times but the windows were reinforced, and there was no one out there for miles.

She could hear the screams from men, women, and children constantly throughout the day. There were sounds where you couldn't understand what was going on, but you know it's vile. She actually tried to stop him several times from going in there but he just puts her to sleep. Over time, as much as she hated to come to terms with it, whatever was happening in that basement began to feel normal. Hearing the sounds and screams just became another part of the day.

She eventually worked up the nerve to go in there with him and watch. Just for the hope of him letting her go. She eventually went and got used to this as well. Although she went down there so many times now, the question is still stuck at the forefront of her mind.

Now, they were sitting together at the bed again eating dinner.

"Chris, about all those people you have in the basement downstairs." she started.

"Yes, princess. What about them?" he responds.

"Why didn't I become one of them?" As soon as she asked, she immediately regretted her question. She may not like what comes next.

"Because, princess, you were different. You were someone I could turn to, you are more than that; like a friend but more. You know where I'm getting at. And princess, you will never leave this place. That's never going to happen, you are going to stay here with me."

Her heart dropped at that statement. That's when she thought that she was never going to leave at least not under his consent, so she just waited. Over time, things changed and she found that eventually she did form feelings toward him. she went out with him, even helped him at the bar. Working there and then looking into the eyes of the same people being brought into that basement being brutalized in front of her eyes again and again, until they died.

"If I'm being honest, I grew into someone who never wanted to leave and one thing led to another. That's when I conceived you, with him being your father. I managed to escape his clutches, with you being left behind. Ronnie, I knew he would never hurt you though. He loved you too much and when I called the authorities on him. I hadn't thought you would be so grim about it.

"I wanted to wait until you were older, but the thought of the bodies stacking up. I just couldn't bear it any longer. I'm sorry." she said.

6

Ronnie was at a complete loss. His mother extended her hand in an effort to comfort him but he backed away. This reminded her of when she first met her father but now, she was the monster. She walked out into the rain, saying she'll be back to restock Ronnie on medical supplies. As Ronnie saw her walk off, he truly thought that he was an offspring brought out to the world by monsters.

He sat beside his wife. She had just gained consciousness yesterday. At the moment, she seemed to be fully speaking to Ronnie.

"Are you sure you don't remember anything from your dream?" Ronnie said.

"For the last time. No, I just remember black and now I'm seeing you here. That's all." Serena said in response.

She stared at him; he was painting beside her and wondered if he was really painting her.

"Hey, let me see the painting." she said.

"You asked at the right time. I just finished it." he said as he turned the painting of her around.

"Whoa! It's you taking care of me and me smiling at you while you do it. I don't think I would be very happy if I knew that it came down to you operating on me when I got hurt."

"You're a very funny woman. Did you know that?" he said. "You should do your own stand up just so I can boo you off the stage."

She burst into laughter and she suddenly winced. Ronnie got up to see what had happened to her.

"Don't be like that caveman. Go back to doing what you were doing in your little lair over there." she said.

"You're being patient with me being away from you now. Not too long ago that you were nasty and irritable about me being away from you." Ronnie said.

Serena's smile then quickly disappeared once he said that. "Yeah, about that, Ronnie. Listen, you don't need to be here if you don't want to. Really, go and get lost in your place." she said.

"No." Ronnie objected. "I..."

He saw Serena's eyes tearing up.

"Ronnie, why are you still here?" she said with her voice cracking.

"Serena, you're hurt, why wouldn't I..."

"That's not what I meant, like....." she pauses for a moment so she wouldn't burst into tears. Why are you doing all this? Why would you put up with me?"

"You're my wife. I have to....."

"Ronnie, stop." she asserted herself as tears rolled down her face. "I've raised my hand againts you, injured you, forced you into sex. You even got fucking raped." She burst into short crying fits. "Why the fuck are you still here?"

"What? Were you trying to push me away?" he asked.

"No Ronnie, I was trying to keep you and keep things the way I wanted to be. I mean, I'm a piece of shit." she retorted. " A fucking monster that's just abused you because I was scared. It's so embarrassing."

"There's nothing to be embarrassed about." Ronnie said, trying to reassure her.

"No Ronnie, I'm talking about you. You! Like, why the fuck would you put yourself through all tha and then just act like everything is fine? Is it just because I abused you?" Serena is starting to get hysterical now. "'Understand me better and get all sympathetic!' It's all excuses for me. You don't even know where the kids are and yet you act like everything is okay."

He leaned in and tried to give her a hug but she put her arm up to stop him from embracing her. He saw her entire face was now red. Her tears streaming constantly down her cheeks.

"Ronnie." she cried out, choking back her tears. "You helped me kill my own father. You took his head off, Ronnie."

Ronnie was at a complete loss of what to say. He knew she was right and it was embarrassing to him as a man who couldn't see it the way she did. The lack of love for himself resulted in this. He sees it now, his wife was a monster.

He had to face the reality of it too. Like mother and father, he too was a monster.

Ronnie was there sitting on the couch, waiting for his mother to show up that day. Today was the day she would restock him with supplies to help Serena, now fully alert but still had to stay in bed.

He waited long, waiting to see his mother walk up to the house today. Then he saw her, his mother was a bit stunned to see her son staring out so menacingly. Gathering herself, she continued inside. Upon entering, she was hesitant to put another step forward. A leg appeared suddenly blocking her way.

"Do you know where he is?" he demanded.

"Um well. Not at the moment. Here are the supplies, you may need......" Isabella responded.

"Where is he staying now,?" Ronnie said, sounding more demanding.

"The old house where you grew up, Ronnie. He's there." she said.

Ronnie then got up and hugged his mother. In shock she dropped the basket of supplies that she was holding and hugged him back. Her eyes burned and started to water, she didn't say a word and just enjoyed the embrace that he was giving her.

Ronnie then walked out and got into his car and drove off.

In the bed, Serena thought about her last moments with Ronnie, just then memories came flashing to her repeatedly.

"You say that I'm not supposed to love you anymore. You did all that to me and it doesn't make sense for me to be continuously doing any of this. It is embarrassing. Yes, you're right." Ronnie breathed out.

"But I'm tired of trying to make sense of everything. Doing what others ask of me because it's better for me to do it this way or that way. I'm just not really happy with any of it. I just want to do things the way I wanted it to be." Ronnie paused, took a deep breath and continued. "Serena, I want you and I don't care how this looks. I really don't."

"I do what I want and what I want is us. It's toxic. It's wrong but I love it and above all, I love you." He held her hand tightly and kissed her.

She couldn't stop thinking of it.

Eventually, she came to terms with it all. The kids were probably better off without her and Ronnie because the sad part of it was that she had to come to terms with the fact that they were all monsters; they were happy that way.

7

Ronnie pulled up in front of the house. Strangely, it was exactly as he remembered it. He wasted no time getting out of the car and going inside.

Once he stepped foot inside, he noticed a trail of meat that led to a room. In the room, he saw Drake's body. His head was missing, a shotgun hung in front of his deceased body. Behind him was a bloody wall with the blood reaching all the way to the ceiling. The trail of meat was from the remnants of his entrails. A collar hung around his neck, burnt to crisp.

He stood there frozen. All of a sudden someone pulled the trigger. *I can picture who would that be,* Ronnie thought.

"Isn't that just something else, Ronnie?"

Ronnie turned to see his father in the wheelchair staring back at him.

"How indecisive some people could be. In the end, although they don't mean it, they end up hurting others around them. Making others look like pawns and fools as consequence." Holman said.

"Look at you." he continued. "Your wife and your kids would be sure to follow in that path too. It's pleasant to know that they will be far away from you but I wouldn't say that I wouldn't have some events planned for them."

Ronnie ran towards his father and without hesitation he punched him with so much force that made him fall out of his wheelchair.

"You're welcome." Chris said.

"Where are my kids?" Ronnie said menacingly.

"One is being made to be my puppet. The other is coming with me, where she and I will be making stories together." Chris answered excitingly.

Ronnie gave him two right hooks. Each punch expressing all his pent up anger. He grabbed his throat and slammed his head straight to the floor.

"I know you've been hurting son. Let it all out." said Chris.

Ronnie gave him a barrage of punches that left his face disfigured. His face was swelling so much, blood covered his whole face. Ronnie's hands bled and were shaking from the beating that he delivered.

"Don't worry, Ronnie. It takes more than that to hurt me." Chris teased.

Ronnie, with all his might punched and stomped his father in the gut. He got a broom and used it to beat him repeatedly. Hearing bones fracture and blood splatter, he continued on until he almost passed out from exhaustion.

"Oh yes. Plenty more than that." his father uttered.

Ronnie grew furious and adrenaline coursed through his veins, giving him more power.

"Tell me, how is your mother doing? I did see her inside your house. She seemed to be out of her wits for a couple of days. I saw that all she needed was a nice big hug from you. Indeed, the expression on her face was so wonderful." Chris inquired.

"You were stalking my house?" Ronnie asked.

"No, no. You see, I was watching my princess as she was out and about. Such a glorious woman, she is." he said.

"You're a sick fuck." Ronnie said to him.

"Ronnie, if that was the case, why don't you do yourself and everyone else a favor then." Chris said, egging him on.

Ronnie slammed Chris against the wall.

"Where the fuck are my kids?!" Ronnie demanded.

"Kill me and then you'll know. Trust me on this. All will be revealed to you if you just kill me." Chris choked out.

"What the fuck are you talking about, huh? Killing you? How is that going to show me where my kids are?" Ronnie pressed on.

"That painting, the one you were finishing before you passed out. Why don't you go ahead and take a look at some of the new art that just got finished? It's one hell of a piece. I'll even let you see what happened to them. It's only fair right? After all, they are your children." he said.

"First you have to kill me. Right here and right now or else you will never see your kids again. After that, I'll go after everyone else. So, if you don't want that to happen, you'll have to kill me. Simple enough, yes?"

Ronnie then grabbed a hammer and whacked until nothing was left but slaughtered meat on the floor.

Upon entering his house, Ronnie went straight to his work room. Serena saw him and grunted as she got out of bed. Her body ached but it was bearable. Ronnie's mother was gone. To where? No one knew.

As Serena continued, the pain eventually went away, and she could walk behind Ronnie with ease now. She followed Ronnie to his work room, where there were new paintings covering the walls.

"Ronnie, how did you paint all this?" Serena said.

"I didn't." Ronnie responded.

The person who showed up that day to get our kids was someone familiar, Ronnie thought.

A fake face showed up with fake memories, it couldn't be helped.

As they looked around, they saw every detail in those paintings. Their daughter, now a woman, is in a bloody mess with a baby being taken away from her. Their son Damien, in the painting he was cage fighting with a little boy named Chris but in parenthesis the letter K was written over the boy's head. Damien was performing several horrid things.

And finally, they both looked at a painting entitled 'Man In Hat'. Pictured was a man who was wearing a hat and holding a little girl, who looked a lot like their daughter.

Serena's blood boiled and Ronnie felt his rage growing at the scene they both saw. He saw his father's face and the picture seemed to come to life. Their daughter seemed real as if they could walk through the frame and hold her. When he touched the painting, his hand became part of the picture. It is as if his consciousness was elevated, he immediately knew what needed to be done.

Serena touched the painting and filled her with knowledge too. His father was teasing them with regards to what was coming.

They knew this had to stop, the end has to be reached.

For the first time ever, Ronnie felt this feeling of this control and resistance. To stand against something, was a feeling that felt so right.

He looked at the wounds she inflicted. Still stunned that he couldn't seem to heal these wounds. An emotional attachment that conflicted him, he was lost now more than ever.

Man In Hat

I sat on the stool, along with everyone else in the saloon; scared and frozen stiff. Staring at the door you couldn't hear anything at all, not a single sound. What you could see was the endless flood of blood that spilled from under the door. I tried not to pay no attention to it and just stared at his hat, a cowboy hat that was a little worn and completely black.

Somehow, I just couldn't ignore it, filling the edge of my mind. I kept my focus on his hat. The blood is still not ceasing. Oh, you just never knew a man can hold that much blood.

I stared intensely at the hat and soon became enamored by it. Endless pitch black that reminded me of him in a good sense. I heard the knob twist and I was brought back to reality. I saw everyone jump in shock, we all turned our focus at the door. He emerged from the open door and I saw him bloodied and beaten very badly.

He walked towards me, his hand stretched out. A man rushed towards him, pinned him against the wall. He looked at the man's face and saw that half of his face was severely burnt. He continued to stare with fear and determination in his eyes. He wanted to give it a shot himself. He pulled out a knife and slowly motioned toward his stomach.

As he continued to motion towards his stomach, the man was shocked and confused. He continued until he heard the knife hit the wall he was pinned to. The only thing his knife did pierce through was the man's bloodstained shirt. He slowly pulled his knife back, still staring at the man who, now with fear in his eyes, slowly backed away.

The man walked towards me again but this time, I reached out towards him, holding out his hat. He picked it from the top and put it on. I glanced at the room before we left and saw the entire scenario. The whole room was red and four bodies lay motionless on the floor.

I made sure to collect the money from the people in the saloon before we left and grabbed the sign that covered our Wanted poster. I stuffed everything in my backpack. The sign said that they are offering a bounty to those who can kill him and would be twice as much if they bring him alive. I knew that it would be a long walk and I was not wrong.

Soon it became dark and it was decided that we should get some sleep. We were in the middle of the desert. This was the best spot, out in the middle of nowhere; where we made holes to rest as we went. I pulled out my shovel and started digging a hole for me to sleep in. MITH used to help me, but after I got the hang of it, I insisted that there wasn't a need for him to do it. From then on he's just been watching me, making sure I do it right. At least that's the only explanation I came up with for his staring before I head into the hole to sleep. That was when I was eight, now I'm ten.

I finally finished and went into the hole with my blanket to sleep. I saw MITH do the same except he lays flat on the ground looking up at the stars. I closed my eyes and slept.

When I woke up, I saw that it's still night out. I poked my head out to see MITH. I continue to look at him. Part of me was still scared of him, he didn't speak and I caught him staring at me at times. Obviously the things that happen to people who challenge him is part of the reason why I'm scared of him, and for him. In my head, I tried to justify it, thinking that they do deserve it in a way. They're criminals after all, but what does that make us? Just part of the scum of society, I guess.

I had so many questions that I wanted to ask him but he's incapable of speaking. He doesn't respond, at all. Something weird then started happening to him, he's shaking. I ran out of my hole to check it, cuts started appearing and they're pouring blood from them. I tried to wipe it away but it's no use, more blood just keeps coming out. Pieces of his face started to fall off

I knew what's happening at least somewhat. It happens every time we do that bounty or when there's an altercation with someone. It would happen seconds, minutes, or even hours after. I pull out my bag of bandages but I know it doesn't really help. Part of me says that I have to do something, even if my efforts are pointless. Soon, I wrapped up his head and just sat there watching him shake.

"Don't worry MITH. I'm here." I said to him.

I put my arms around him and stayed with him for the rest of the night, feeling him bleed through the bandages and soaking me with blood. I felt his whole body come apart. It's as if the whole night was a complete blur. I didn't get much sleep that night, but I am not entirely awake either. I felt movement when he woke up. He went right to filling up that hole that I dug.

This too, was a ritual he did alone rather than to have me do it. In fact, he wants me at a distance when doing this. I really can't imagine why though.

He took off the bandages and is completely healed at least to a certain degree. He still has the holes burned in his abdomen.

I was happy to see that he was alright. I really should be used to this by now, but when it's happening, I would still get so paranoid. He gave me my backpack and blanket. It's only when I saw my hands that I realized that we're both covered in dried blood.

I puzzled at it for a moment, trying not to freak out but MITH seemed to pay no attention to it at all. As soon as he started walking, I started walking.

I looked up and saw him. I wondered, what he might be thinking or how he feels about some things but he also does seem to keep going with conviction and that reassures me no matter what the situation is.

Eventually we reached another town not far off. It was completely empty. We found some water and used it to clean ourselves and later, I washed our clothes. I did find myself a little curious about the fact that the whole town is completely empty.

I'm sure MITH does too, but he doesn't seem in the least bit bothered by it. He hung his shirt up to dry, sat on the stairs and watched it getting blown in the air. I did clean myself too then washed and dried my clothes in some machine I found. I joined him on the stairs and watched his shirt swim in the wind.

It's sort of hard to remember the time when I first met MITH; he didn't talk and I was with both of my parents when he appeared. I did know that I was with a family at one point but didn't remember exactly when I met MITH. For as long as I can remember, I've been with him. I did remember the time when I came up with his name. Really, I couldn't think of anything else so I eventually called him MITH; an acronym for Man In The Hat.

I actually saw his holes up close. The large one was in the middle of his abdomen, big enough to put my head through. Another was on his chest where his heart should be, it looked like a slanted diamond. The wound would probably fit two of my hands through. All the rest of the holes just sort of filled up his body, big enough to where you could visibly see them.... and through them.

His half-burnt face was unrecognizable while the other half, you can only distinguish his eye out of it.

I looked at him seeing how he's so lost and transfixed in that shirt. Maybe just lost in thought, similar to how I get lost in his hat.

"You know, MITH, they have dryers and washers round here if you feel any use for them." I said.

No response from him as if it's like I hadn't said anything.

"Well, the more you know." I said.

I joined him in staring at the shirt. It's really peaceful the way the gentle air flows through it. I stared out into the distance and saw something moving. I started to move but MITH stopped me before I could stand up to my feet.

He saw what I'm seeing, he stood up and walked towards it. He motions for me to go into the house. I went in and found a window where I could clearly see him. As he came in close proximity to it, it exploded.

I jolted back as the shockwave pushed me backwards. I regained myself however, and saw MITH in pieces, his body parts burning in the fire.

I've seen this a thousand times now. He'll make it through, he always does. I ducked my head down to avoid the scene.

"He's fine now, lift your head and he'll be alright." I said to myself, as I eventually got the audacity to lift my head up and still saw parts of him being burnt to a crisp.

His hat. Where's his hat? I frantically looked around and found it sitting on the porch.

I have to go and get it, I thought. Without thinking I ran outside and picked up the hat and rushed back inside. I looked back and couldn't see him anywhere. The fire kept spreading, then I heard another bomb went off as the flames rose even higher. I felt the heat against the window and began to sweat. I ran to the other side of the house.

I got to the other side, it's blocked with fire as well. I ran to the bedroom and closed the door. The smoke came in and I soon started coughing. It almost became impossible to breathe. I heard more explosions go off which made the whole house shake. I started to suffocate, I fell off the bed but still held his hat close to me. My eyes started to water and my vision started to go black. I saw the door burst open, he stood there, barely being put together but still falling apart in other places.

He wrapped me up using the bed cover. I could only guess what's happening, I could feel him pick me up and carry me. I thought I felt him jump and crash through a window. I felt him carry me closer to something warm.

I held the hat a lot more tightly as I tried to find an opening in the covers. I eventually did and placed a part of my head through and saw the situation in front of him. He has nowhere to go, nowhere but through the flames. He made eye contact with me then placed the cover over me again.

I could feel his limp body moving through the flames and me along with him. I placed my hands over my mouth so I won't scream. The intense pain I felt and the heat were completely unbearable but holding the hat and staring at it helped me through it. We eventually got out of the fire but he kept walking for so long.

He fell over and the covers that wrapped around me came undone and I saw him struggling to pick himself up as trucks came up and people stepped out and started shooting at him. With the first shot, he fell to the ground but they still kept shooting him. I saw him turn into smaller pieces, again to what might be considered as minced meat.

Eventually there was silence and I knew what's about to happen next. Some of them burned, other parts fell off and the rest turned into chunks of meat. The look of terror in their faces was both satisfying and hard to watch. Seeing the burnt decayed skin, hearing appendages hit the ground and the smell of fresh flesh; was a sight so horrid in my eyes.

There was silence once again and I saw MITH form up again but then just as soon as I could start to recognize his burnt face, he fell apart again. He started to regain his form but just fell to nothing but shredded meat again, this process happened again and again until he regenerated to his full self.

He started to move, however his arm fell off and another one grew to take its place. I see the arm lay there and decay. MITH still continues to walk until his leg fell off and he fell. His flesh came off the bone effortlessly and both bone and flesh decay.

As he walked with a dreadful limp, pieces of him continued to fall apart while he healed. The flesh was bloody bright red and it fell off him in huge chunks. I could hear his bone break every time it cracks, it's so loud and unnerving.

I could actually see the flesh grow back around his bone only to decay and fall off again.

An endless pour of blood comes out from his body. I heard him choke and gurgle in his own blood. The choking became more unbearable when it started to come out of his mouth and it didn't stop. His abdomen exploded and left his guts hanging out. I looked behind us and saw a long trail of blood and guts. I looked down at the burnt hat and went on autopilot as my mind got lost in it.

I finally started to notice that MITH was no longer bleeding and was no longer falling apart anymore, he's alright now. Just when I noticed that, I took my mind off the hat and looked at him. My vision became blurry and I blacked out.

I woke up to see a man digging again; it was MITH, burying something again. The sight of him looked fine, at least his usual self. He's finally done and walked away. I ran to him, joining him again on the walk. We soon went off and saw a store. Obviously, he can't go into places like this unless he wants to make money on his bounty. Instead, he trusted me to go in and see what I can buy for the both of us.

Okay, so he needs new clothes, his usual attire should do. I looked back at the entrance to see that he was no longer there. I wondered where he went but something was telling me that this was nothing to worry about.

I found a cart and picked up boots, blue jeans and a buttoned up, long sleeved dark grey colored shirt. On my way around, I saw a library section, or maybe not entirely a library. It could be a just place that sold books. I saw one about a dragon, another about a princess and a final one about a boy and his dog.

Someone tried to approach me but paused and went in the opposite direction. Something weird tends to happen every time I notice them. They would be having this surprised look on their face then change the direction of where they were headed. I think I noticed that feeling too. Almost as if I'm being coerced not to interact with them.

I headed over to the checkout counter and saw the cashier, checked out then I headed outside. I saw him standing in the same spot before I went in.

He started to walk again once I got closer to him, we immediately headed off. As I looked far off in the distance, we seemed to be going to a mountainous area. We then stopped for the night and once I dug my hole, we finally settled in. I pulled out a book for MITH. I loved the art of the dragon on the cover. It's so beastly, the way it conveys him like a monster.

"Hey MITH. Wait, I have something to show you." I rushed towards him with the book.

I saw him lying on the ground, looking up at the sky, in wonder as always. I sat beside him, opened the book and began reading.

"There once was a lonely dragon that only wanted solitude and peace in the quiet grass where it rested and slept." I look at the picture that made the dragon look so peaceful in his setting of flowers and grass, the art here made my heart feel so very warm.

"He found it." I started to read. "In the place that was once his home, now surrounded in the plains of grass that stretched on as far as his eyes could see. But it was not always quiet, as the peaceful light of the moon was broken by the fire that laid waste to the land. It scorched the dragon's back and part of its wing very badly."

"The angry townspeople did this while it slept. The dragon tried to fly away but the fire had burned part of its wing to the bone making it unable to fly. So, it struggled to make its way out of the flames path. The dragon struggled to flap its wings and soon he could fly again and this time it flew far off until he came upon another open grassfield. At last, another open field that wouldn't be disturbed by anyone. The dragon lay there until it felt something scratching at its belly. When it looked down it saw that there were more angry townspeople that went and cut at it."

"The dragon tried to run away but its stomach fell out and was dragging it along the plains, making it bloody. The dragon however did not stop until the townspeople were out of sight. It saw another moment to rest and it collapsed to the ground."

"The anger of the townspeople was clearly tied into the history of this dragon. For you see, this creature was not of the violent kind for it only wanted peace. But as it slept and rested, the fire within its body released a poisonous heat that warmed the rest of the land. Giving way to disease and some of the townspeople died of heat stroke and severe illness."

"Given very few options, they opted to kill the creature to make sure their suffering wouldn't happen again at the hands of this great beast."

"So, it has come to this, the dragon is now unable to move it's left wing. It looked at its wing as dead weight. The dragon felt the bone weakening and then felt it strain as its skin tore, soon, there was a loud crack. A much longer cracking sound was heard, the bone was breaking, the skin continued to tear until his left wing finally came off."

"The dragon had lost its ability to fly."

"The dragon now unable to move due to heavy blood loss, could only watch as his bloody smell attracted other creatures that feasted on him. With the amount of flesh chewed from his body, finally it released heat, hot enough to send the creatures running."

"However, the dragon didn't have the strength to tolerate this heat as he did before. He caught fire and the townspeople gathered in celebration as the dying dragon was now taking its final breath."

"The dragon closed its eyes. It saw a warm light and in this warm light he felt as if he was in the grass resting and sleeping quietly. It knew that it would be at peace again soon and so it rejoiced in silence. A place where it could no longer bother anyone else and no one can bother it."

I paused for a moment and looked back at the cover of the book. I could see the dragon in someone's perspective, someone who perceived this creature as a monster for it destroyed his loved ones. I supposed that feeling was in a way justified, although the situation was a bit unfair for the dragon.

I looked at MITH after I placed the book down and saw that he's looking straight at me. However, it's not that lost look he usually got on his face. It's that focused look as if I'm the only person here and he's studying me enough to make me uneasy.

He then turned his eyes toward the book and stared at that for some time before returning his gaze to me.

"Um. MITH, are you alright? What's wrong?" I questioned.

He responded by handing me the shovel; he wanted me to be in the hole now.

The silence this time was different. Although it was just as quiet, he stared with a different purpose now, studying me very thoroughly before I went into the hole. I crawled inside the hole and lay there faking sleep. I still feel him watching me as if waiting for something or thinking of something. I didn't know why, but he never ceased to stare at me.

I honestly couldn't say if he was still staring at me anymore and I couldn't sleep. My mind was becoming restless, curiosity eventually won over me and I turned around. I got the answer to my question. There he was staring at me, and for the first time ever I saw some intent of violence upon his face.

I froze for a second, mind racing, trying to think of something. The only thing that came to mind were the books that I had yet to read. Though not a smart choice, it's something that had definitely seemed to have sparked his interest.

"MITH, would you like to read another book? I don't think that I could sleep without another story." I said with a tinge of fear in my voice.

I reached for my bag and saw that it's not here in my hole with me. I climbed out of my hole, still trying to ignore his stare. I searched for it and I saw that it's far off from us. I decided not to question this and just moved to get it.

Something in me made me move rather slowly, I felt as if I was halfway between frozen and having the courage to move. Not daring to look back, I continued to look at my bag and saw that all three of the books were still in there. I then walked back, staring at the ground until I reached my hole.

I pulled out one of the books. Story about a princess that seemed really gorgeous on the cover, showing a kingdom bright and vibratrant. Showing the princess sitting at the back overlooking everything.

"There was once a young woman who had a father and a mother. She was very loved by both of her parents. She did as her mother told and followed as her father said. She respected them both. While doing her daily chores around the house, she saw a crow and stared into its eyes, it stared back into hers."

"She saw the crow and how it looked down upon her and curious as to why it looked at her. *What could that crow be thinking about?*. she wondered. She continued on to her day and eventually night fell. She looked out her window, at the crow who was still staring back at her."

I think I can relate to how this girl is feeling now, I thought as I continued to read.

"The girl thought of why the crow still stared. *Oh, it just looked so precious*, the girl thought. She waved at it and waited if it would acknowledge her by waving back. It didn't however, the girl stared at it again until the crow went to sleep. She too, then went to sleep."

"She woke up the next day and still saw the crow outside sleeping. She ran outside to the crow and picked it up. The crow woke to the girl, and astonishingly it didn't fly away. Instead, it felt comforted around the arms of the young girl and rested its head on her bicep."

"The girl then disappeared for the rest of the day not alerting anyone of where she was going. The father and mother were worried sick and searched relentlessly for their only daughter. The father and mother both grew paranoid and depressed on what could have happened to their daughter. The sadness sent them into illness."

"One day the daughter did return with the crow. Her parents who were understandably angry, scolded their daughter. They demanded a reason for her sudden disappearance. She cried and showed them the crow and they understood."

"They decided to keep it for their daughter's sake and it lived with them as a pet. Their illness then went away as their daughter was now back safe into their lives once more."

"However, their daughter grew lazy with the chores. She did not spend time with them but with the crow that she would not go anywhere without. This worried them as she became secluded from the rest of the world. Not going outside, except to give the crow a bathroom break."

"They tried to take it forcibly away from her but she would yell and scream. Reasoning of course, did not help. The little girl said that she couldn't leave her child alone. That turned the matter into a more serious one. The mother waited until her daughter had slept and went to the crow and grabbed it but it cawed loudly, waking the girl. The girl told her mother to stop but the mother persisted, the father then came in to hold his daughter back."

"The mother threw the crow outside but it flew its way back into the house, straight to the girl and started attacking the father. Who in defense, whacked it to the ground making his daughter scream. The crow then grew fiercer, attacking the man. Digging its talons into his face and pecking at his head, giving the crow a bloody beak. The mother then grew angry, grabbed a broom and beat the crow into the wooden floor until it ceased to move."

"The daughter, still struggling, began attacking her father to get to the crow. The father who was blinded by the blood on his face could only hold her tightly."

"The mother went to throw the beaten crow in the dumpster. Locking the door to the house as she stepped in. The father then disciplined his irate daughter who then went quiet. The father then walked to the bathroom to clean his wounds, and the worried wife helped her husband."

"The next day, the father's face was heavily bandaged while the daughter did not speak since last night. The mother tried to talk to her daughter, but it was pointless as the girl didn't respond. The father tried to explain but it was the same result: it was as if they were talking to a brick wall."

"Later that day, the girl sat in her room staring outside. She couldn't believe her eyes. It was the crow beaten and bruised. She went to the door, but it was locked. The father rested with his wounds but the mother was out and about. The girl didn't care as she broke one of the windows and the crow flew in once again."

"The mother heard this and went to investigate. The daughter grabbed the crow and went to the kitchen. She looked at how beaten the crow was, her blood boiled. The girl then grabbed a knife, gripping it hard. The mother followed her daughter into the kitchen. She quickly wheeled around and brutally stabbed her mother."

"Bleeding to death, her mother said, "We were trying to help you." and she breathed her last."

"The girl then went to the room where her father was and stabbed his neck and face repeatedly. He couldn't say anything while he stared at his daughter choking on his own blood until he stopped moving."

"The little girl finally saw the house as her own now, with her little child that was a crow. In her eyes it was like a big castle where she and the crow could do whatever they wanted. Like a princess in a big kingdom that was all hers."

I put the book down slowly and looked at the ground. *This was definitely not a smart idea,* I thought.

"MITH, I'm not really all that sleepy anymore." I saw him get up, dug in another hole and he filled up the same hole with dirt. He then began to walk off.

I then began quickly stuffing everything into my bag and went after him until I caught up. We continued to walk through the desert until we reached a house in the middle of nowhere. The walk was a long one and had me sweating and I spotted a couch to where I jumped on and laid out.

I'm so tired from not sleeping last night. This is just right, I thought to myself as I let my eyelids fall and finally rest. I saw MITH sitting on a chair staring at the distance at the front door.

I tried not to worry since the last time that something went bad, everything came out just fine. I just needed to go with the flow of things and relax when things were at ease. MITH always came out fine and I too, always came out with his hat with me intact, all thanks to him.

I closed my eyes once more and felt the comfort the couch gives. Hearing a sound, I sprung up and it seemed like someone was yelling. I got up and it's MITH who I saw getting attacked by angry townspeople. I tried to move but I was stuck. Others were holding me down to the couch.

"Let him die! You need to be my little girl again." a woman said.

They impaled him on a stake and hoisted him up, displaying him like a trophy. I tried to struggle again but a man joined to hold me down as well.

"Listen to your mother, doll. This needs to be done." he said.

"No!" I shouted and continued to thrash harder until I saw that I was still laying on the couch.

Was I dreaming? I thought.

That's when I heard a splash. I turned and it was MITH bleeding again. I went to him with my bag but he gestured his hand, signaling for me to stay away. He's taking something out from his neck. It was a huge and long wooden stake that was almost the length of his arm.

He struggled to breathe with a huge hole where his throat was supposed to be. He looked at other parts of his body where other stakes seemed to have been pierced. His legs, arms, and face all seemed to have been successfully pierced with accuracy. Each stake he took out, his blood flowed like a water faucet being turned on.

He fell over toward the opening of the door. I rushed for him to make sure he was okay. He sat up against the wall of the doorway and stared outside. There were piles upon piles of dead bodies that littered an empty desert.

I gazed out and saw that it was completely endless. I heard a gun being cocked behind my head and MITH stood up, still hurting but looks like he almost healed. I was pulled back by a woman that was shaking with nervousness, holding a pistol aimed at my head.

MITH pulled a stake from his foot and stared at the woman. He slit his own throat and blood oozed from the deep cut. Then as if instantaneously, I felt warm drops of blood on my forehead MITH then reached inside of his wounded neck and took out his cervical spine. The woman's cervical spine dislodged itself and flew over my head right in front of my feet; the woman fell over to my right.

Suddenly, I looked at MITH and noticed where his hat was, it was right on the couch where I placed it. MITH gurgled as blood poured from where his neck was supposed to be and his head struggled to keep stable as if he had no bone to keep it steady. He then fell over paralyzed from it and started to heal once again.

I ran for the hat and grabbed it. Honestly, seeing MITH's head bobble back and forth was somehow frightening and funny at the same time, I smiled a little.

Just go with the flow, I thought as he started to move again. We continued to wait there and I tried to sleep again but to no avail. We soon started to move onwards again after we looted some of the bodies, of course. The walking resumes, but I however felt a little better and a little more energetic thanks to the rest I got earlier.

As we moved, I thought of what just transpired at the house we were at. We just got attacked and those people were coming into our house. *Were there really people holding me back?* I thought again. Listen to my mother, this has to happen, the phrases kept spinning around in my head.

Those weren't hired guns like earlier either but everyday towns people. They were actually impaling him on stakes. That was different than before, it's like in the stories that I read. *No part of it had to be a dream,* I thought. This was all so very confusing, it made my head hurt just by thinking of it. We ended up at the foot of the mountains and trekked upwards from there.

MITH was covered in blood again, it's useless to buy him new clothes if he would just mess it up. We then found a spot to where we would finally rest. Every time we stopped, it's so great to just fall flat on the ground and stay there. Just being content with the whole thing.

Although I had to admit that it was cold, I took off my shoes and saw that my feet were swollen and bleeding slightly, it really hurts. But as much as it hurts, it feels great.

There's no way anyone would come up here and take us on. At least, I would think so. I slept more peacefully now and woke up to see it's nighttime. MITH laid out and staring up at the stars. *That sleep was beautiful,* I thought. My feet felt much better too even though it is much colder during night time.

Those stories kept swarming my head and I kept thinking about the last story that I haven't read yet. It's driving me mad, how I couldn't think of anything else. So, I battled with the thought for another hour. It still hasn't gone away yet, so I finally got my bag out.

"Hey MITH. It's time for another story." I said.

I knew this wasn't in the least sense very smart, but it's probably the only way I can get closure on this.

I knew that MITH would start acting hostile toward me but I could only hope that this story wasn't like the others. Even if that was only a slight chance, so slight that one couldn't even hope for it.

"There was a boy that lived in the middle of nowhere and with nothing to do, he explored the wilderness in search of activity. He would normally spend his time climbing trees and messing with animals. As the boy grew, he became more bored and sought new activities to do."

"He eventually had gotten a couple of dogs from the kennel. He didn't take care of them very well other than feeding them, of course. When he chose them, he wanted to make sure that they were as big and as vicious as possible. The reason for this was so that when a couple of hikers or people came by, the dogs would maul them."

Well, this went south quickly, I thought as I considered putting the book down. But I was already into the book and might as well finish it up now.

""The backyard was filled with bones of the people the dogs devoured. The man was highly entertained as he would watch with a smile on his face at how the dogs ate them alive. At how violently dogs bit and slammed their victims and how they fought over their victims' flesh."

"It was all so satisfying to him, he laughed at how ridiculously fun it was to watch this. One day, they went on the hunt for more victims to send to the slaughter that were his dogs. He couldn't find anyone out in the woods but he did find a smaller dog."

"The dog looked frightened and shook at the sight of the man who advanced toward him. The dog was extremely small and looked almost like a rat. The man picked the dog up; he would have to settle on this for today. Frustrated, he threw the dog in the backyard and sat in his chair and drank his beer. The dogs emerged from their own parts of the yard and surrounded the tiny dog."

"They then leapt forward to him, tearing his flesh, tossing him around like a ragdoll. The sacred and frightened dog had the will to live as the world would let things be possible. He fought back such a ferocity that was more violent than the bigger dogs could muster. The tiny dog looked more like a rat which tore the bigger dogs apart."

"He tore them piece by piece, exposing their bone, tearing one's leg off and having one bleed out from its head. They eventually cowered at the smaller dog but that did not stop him. He then continued to maul at them with such viciousness, the man was left stunned."

"At the end of it, the small dog licked at the bones of the bigger dogs that he killed. The man was impressed at what happened. The next day he found out that it was not a human but a wolf and led him inside the backyard. It was as if he couldn't believe it, the wolf didn't even put up a fight instead it ran away."

"Over the years the man grew fond of the dog. This one dog would maim anything that the man placed inside his backyard. In return, the dog grew to trust the man and the man took care of the dog as if it were his own. One day when he went outside and into the woods,he stumbled upon a group of people that recognized him and they attacked."

"This man had upset the town with his rapes, murders and robberies. This man was clearly frowned upon. Immediately after committing a crime, the man would flee into the woods. Thus, the town decided along with the law enforcement that this man had to be put down after so many acts of violence. So, a search party for the man was made. Only this search party was aimed to kill."

"He ran for his life trying to escape them but they wouldn't let him be. He had to go to his house where he would hide. They still followed, watching him as he entered his house. The dog saw his owner run in, and saw the group of people coming after him."

"The dog then lunged at the first person he saw, and began to attack the rest of the angry mob. The angry mob was in horror but were desperate to kill the man who slaughtered their loved ones. So the dog fought even after his teeth went dull and broke. Using anything and everything else he had, including his claws."

"When they went dull and tore from his paw, he went back to biting even after his mouth bled. The man stepped out after everything went quiet, and saw the front yard littered with bodies. He then had seen what the dog sacrificed for these littered bodies."

"The man then cared for the dog and once it was done, they both continued to live there. The dog patrolled the house, guarding it from anyone and everyone that stepped foot near it. He had plenty of food to eat with all the decayed bodies."

"The man then continued to seek his entertainment and they both stayed even after their deaths. For that was there one and only place they both knew as it would be there in purgatory, heaven, and hell."

"See. MITH? This had a good ending, sort of, the bad guys won." I laughed nervously as I closed the book.

I looked back at the cover and saw them and the bodies in the background.

Something just came to mind and she looked at the title, no title, no author, no illustrator. I looked at the other books and it was the same thing. *How peculiar,* I thought.

I could see MITH staring off at the distance he was breathing more heavily than usual.

"MITH, why don't you sit down? You look tired."

He didn't seem to hear me properly, he leaned on his knees. I began to worry again and felt like I'd upset him from reading the story.

"Is it because of the story MITH? I'm sorry. I probably shouldn't have done that." I said.

I hated it when this happened. He's been acting out of place for a while now eversince I read those stories, definitely a dumb move.

Something was crawling all throughout his body. I saw how his skin stretched to form what appeared to be a creature crawling inside him. It stopped in one part of his body and I heard a bone crack and his insides being torn. It looked like it was eating him from the inside.

He started bleeding and it busted out from the right side of his chest. They created another hole went inside, it busted out from his back and crawled around. It was hard to tell what it was, it was black and wet, dripping blood from itself.

It looked like a black shapeless blob with arms and legs that walked on all fours. It soon turned into a woman and cried for me.

"My little girl." she said. "Please just let it be."

"Wait, you're my….."

I stopped and saw someone else. I couldn't say if it's true but they looked so familiar that they had to be.

"Please, darling. We're trying to help you." he said.

Frightened, I backed up, unsure of what to do. I looked towards MITH and saw him walking towards me. The two people noticed him and their faces turned from sorrow to pure hate in an instant.

They attacked him and screamed at him.

"Stay away from her!" the man yelled.

No!, I thought as I lunged on top of the man.

"Get off him!" I yelled.

I bit his ear and he cried out. He turned and threw me to the ground. I spat a piece of his ear out.

"We're trying to help you, to show you what he truly is." he said desperately.

"Get away from us!" I yelled back at him.

"Hold her down. You have to see how this fucker is gonna get this." the woman said.

The woman grabbed a rock and beat MITH's face in and he fell backward. I tried to stop the woman but the man held me back.

She continued to beat his face with the rock as MITH's blood covered her face. She held his head up forcing him to face me.

"Look at my daughter! Look at what you did! She doesn't even know who you truly are!" she yelled.

"Gotten her in your shit and for what?" the man said. "She's been through hell scared stiff and it's because of you and your fucking ass!"

She continued to beat his face until her husband bled from his head.

"Ronnie, no!" she said. She ran to him as the man let go of me.

124

I went to MITH, he suddenly pulled out a stake and gutted himself. The man soon had a little cut that turned deep and had his intestines hanging.

"Stop!" she said desperately. Her face changed to shock and disbelief as she turned to him.

"What do you want from me?" she said.

"Darling, he could make this much worse if he wanted. He could make it hurt, just do it. This isn't the time." the man said, comforting her.

She cried as she reached for his guts and grabbed his blood-soaked intestines. She wrapped them around his neck to choke him. He eventually passed out and the woman sobbed madly.

"You're simply just pure evil." she said.

"We'll get you back and have all the time in the world to take it slow." she said menacingly.

She smiled as she and the man both turned back into black blobs and crawled back into MITH's body. MITH was shaking severely.

"Please, MITH. Just sit down." I said. He sat and stared at the sun and I on the other hand was at a loss. I stared into the distance until my mind would clear and finally put together what I just saw.

2

My mind still wandered back from what just transpired the other day. MITH still seemed to have not recovered yet. *All the time in the world to take it slow,* that statement continues to echo in my mind. Could that be what's happening to MITH?

I continued to stare out into the distance. What was that? Who were they? That was so different from anything we faced before. I could hear MITH's flesh tearing again. I glanced in his direction again and immediately looked away.

"I want to talk." I said. He ignored me.

"I want to talk." I said again, louder this time. "MITH let them out, please. Just please, let them out now."

MITH looked up at me and soon he stopped shaking. I start seeing them crawl under his skin and shoot out from his body. However, they made sure to be a good distance away from MITH when they took form.

"Oh sweetie, you've finally called out for us." the mother said, facing me.

MITH stood on my left and the two people who are my self-proclaiming parents, stood on my right. They wanted to lure me away from MITH.

"I wanted to talk." I said, looking at the both of them. "Who are you guys?" I asked defensively.

"You should know by now dear. Though, you couldn't feel us inside your head." the man said.

"Well, of course, she can. She's linked to that filthy wretch laying about in his mess!" the woman shouted.

"Stop calling me 'dear' and I'm the one you're talking to, not him." I demanded.

"No, darling, we might as well be talking to the two of you at the same time." the man said.

"What are you getting at?" I questioned.

"Listen." the man demanded. "The only way for you to understand, is for us to let us show you."

"Yes, that's right. Just come here and we'll show you." the woman said.

"No, I'm fine over here." I say stepping back.

"Please, just trust us and it will be a lot clearer. Please." the man pleaded.

"You think of him as an angel, do you?" she said with great distaste. "Well, why don't you go and dig that hole up right beside where he's lying."

"Go on, we won't move a muscle. After all we're just trying to convince you of what he really is, darling." the man said, egging me on.

I stepped back and stared at them and saw the shovel right beside MITH. Who was now sitting against a rock, staring at me as I gripped the shovel. I looked back at the two people who called themselves my parents and saw that they really haven't moved a muscle.

I began digging and periodically glanced up to see that the two were still in the exact same spot. Then I looked at MITH, whose face was staring at the spot that I was digging. It was like he knew there's something there, too. I eventually hit something and I looked down.

I began to dig with my hands and I saw that it was a body. I vomited a little in my mouth.

"Keep digging and you'll see." the woman said.

I peeked towards where the face was and I finally see it now, the body and face. "It's me." I said.

"Please, just come here," the woman said.

I looked at MITH and he only stared back at me blankly.

"I don't understand," I said. I backed away from the hole and towards the center again.

"Oh, look at you, darling. How you matured so much in that little amount of time." she said.

"She's right, dear. Such good vocabulary in just a few moments." the man said, giving me clues as to how weird that was.

"What are you talking about? I've always been able to talk like this." I responded.

"Of course. Yes, you have. That's because you're older than you think, at least not consciously." the woman said.

The voices are becoming familiar now and somehow soothing. The woman took one step towards me, but I didn't back up. I held my head because I could feel my vision spinning. I felt the woman put her hands on my head.

My vision faded to black as I collapsed to the ground, before I was fully aware of what was going on, I blacked out.

I awoke to find myself in a house laying on a bed. So comfortable, I thought. Then I looked out and saw a house across the street. I became fixated on it but I quickly turned my attention away and went downstairs.

"Momma." I say worryingly.

"Yes? I'm right here, darling." she responded.

Running, I went to hug her tightly, gripping my mother's legs.

"Oh, what's wrong sweetie? You seem a little spooked." she said.

"I don't know. It just seems like I've been away for a while now." I said looking up at her.

Her mother smiled the biggest smile saying, "Well, you're here now sweetie. Now sit down and eat."

I did as she said and went to hop on a chair. I stared outside and saw the house again. *That's strange,* I thought. The house seemed to be in an entirely new place.

My mind must just be a bit hazy from the morning. Once I finish eating, I'm still looking at the house, not taking my eyes off it. My mother must have noticed this, so she asked a question.

"Something's got your attention, darling?" she asked as she looked outside.

Once she glanced at it, an expression of shock came over her and she quickly shut the window then closed the curtains. Leaning over the curtain she seemed to try and regroup herself. Without saying a word, she sat back down at the table and continued eating.

Footsteps were coming from upstairs; it was my father. "Hey there, what's going on?" he asked.

"Nothing, daddy. Just eating."

My mother then looked relieved at the sight of him. "Hey there, to you too, sweetie" he said, kissing my mother.

"So darling, have you had any bad dreams lately?" he said.

"No, not lately." I said hesitantly. "Hey, I was wondering. Who lives in that house across the street from us?"

They both looked up at me with surprise.

"So soon." the man said. "Listen honey, some very dangerous people live over there. It's important that you don't go anywhere near that house."

"The less you know, the better it would be, darling." my mother said. "Well could I go outside for a bit after breakfast."

Her face twitches as she says "Of course, dear."

"Just make sure to clean your room and do the dishes first."

"Yes, ma'am." I responded.

I went outside only after doing all of my chores. I was thinking of the house the whole time and now it seemed like it's just drawing me on more. It felt as if someone was calling to me or something was pulling me to it.

I looked around and I didn't see my mother or father, so I beelined and ran through the gate, leaving it wide open. Going to the house, I felt my legs burn but I kept running until I was at the doorstep. Surprisingly the door was left unlocked.

The feeling made me more curious as if someone was teasing me to step inside. Luring me in every direction I turned, whatever it was that's guiding me forward. I heard crying that's coming from behind one of the doors. I saw that it led downstairs.

It was dark but I could still somehow see but I could hardly make anything out.

Slowly my eyes started to adjust and I could see everything more clearly. I saw the source of the crying, a small boy, who was completely emaciated. The sight of him made me sick, his expression made me scared and everything began to go dark again.

I saw nothing but black and the cold made me start to shake senselessly. Everything stayed silent for a moment and then a gunshot was heard. I looked down and saw a book that I had gotten from the store. I thought, *No that couldn't be it. I only got here, this was different.*

I looked at the book and it opened by itself. There was another story here about a boy. A boy who was identical to the one I just saw, I began to read.

A boy was trapped inside a box, struggling to get out and to break free but to no avail. He continued until his muscles ached and he could barely move. Before he took his last breath, two hands grabbed him and freed him from the box.

The boy thankfully went on his way until he stumbled to find himself in another box. A box more horrid in design and a lot more uncomfortable. The boy struggled even harder to get free. Hands bloodied beating at its walls, muscles now cramping with every movement. He feels his breathing and collapses, but just before his last breath, two hands grabbed him and freed him from his prison once again.

The boy although grateful had begun to think. He soon came to the conclusion that another box should be near. With a hot head and feeling as little as a worm, he trapped himself in the worst box yet. Sure enough, the hands came again but the boy hissed back at them. Making them go away. Now with hands turned raw from constant beating, tears fell from his eyes, the pain made him go mad.

His head dented from the constant head butting in desperation of trying to leave. Bones breaking from the constant mad dashing against the wall, trying to escape. The boy felt his lungs now bleeding and with one cough of blood he took his last breath and closed his eyes in contentment of what he had done.

Upon completing the passage, several images flashed before me. At the sight of them, my knees began to buckle and all the air was taken away from me instantly. Still, I struggled to stand and began breathing deeply trying to catch my breath.

"My boy." I called out.

A sudden rush of anxiety filled my body. *Now what?* I thought. A sudden need to see someone who was trapped, a bloodied baby. I tried to focus my mind, brushing those disturbing images out of my mind.

I turned to the next page and began to read. I didn't know why I continued, whether it's curiosity or something else but a feeling washed over me, urging me to keep reading. Like a silent voice telling me to do so, an unknown force of some kind.

As I began reading my eyes went red with strain and tears started streaming down my face. An unknown fear now made my body shake but I continued, only caring for what I was reading. A strong urge to reveal something, making me complete again.

A crawler was born in the midst of darkness. He struggled and tried but failed every time. In this life, he found that he couldn't thrive but he weighed his options only as he laid down and cried. He found a prison and the conditions were scary, then it struck; an idea was ready.

If it were to spend a hundred days in this prison then it would have no problem in this darkness. He then went forward and began his trial, determined to take the first step of a grueling mile.

In the middle of this execution, he then found another institution. This prison was not as bad as it may seem, the other made it look like a wonderful dream. In this new foundation, he is in a less diabolical situation, he felt safe.

Just in his view, however, came a new endeavor. An endless wasteland, a hundred days there, would be a great deal to bear. He ran to this new treat, only thinking of how wonderful and neat it was. But not even a second longer, and his eyes begin to wander. He looked at this hell, and thought about the wonderful tale it would tell.

He started this and was lost in his bliss, finding comfort now. He soon would find the worst place for his head to bow. Never ending in this quest even after being laid to rest.

I began to hear footsteps around me, a boy who's naked and bloody came from the dark. He had serious lacerations all over his body and several parts of his forehead showed exposed bone. He was soaked in blood, still bleeding profusely. He stepped toward me reluctantly, he began to shake more with every step as if he's scared of me. As he came closer he began to whimper. I wanted to step back, but I hesitated to do so.

This feeling that felt so familiar, an urge so strong, as if yelling at me to not only stay but walk to him as well. I didn't retreat, neither did I move forward. I just stayed completely still. The boy was right in front of me now but he didn't look up.

Instead he stared at my legs. He put one hand up and touched it. His hand was very cold at the touch. As he tried to persist, his shaking got worse but soon went away. He then slowly embraced me and hugged my leg. His grip was tight and got tighter with every second. I tried to pry him away but he grabbed my hand and played with my fingers.

I guess this was better than the death grip he had on my leg. He then started to tug at me, leading me towards a direction. As uncomfortable as I was with this boy, a feeling of trust was urging me to follow him and besides he was my only point of direction in this whole place. I really didn't have much of a choice.

3

The mouse poked his head out once and had a second glance at it all; he saw the cat staring out the window so peacefully. It had no care in the world. The mouse wanted to join the cat, giving it some company.

He scurried over to the cat and made his way right beside her. He made out a little squeak to get her attention. The cat jumped up at the sound and turned her head. At the sight of the mouse, the cat clawed at him, giving a hiss as the mouse ducked out of the way barely missing her claws.

The cat was blind with fury at the sight of this mouse; her instinct was that it was its enemy and that it would burden her own life if she did not destroy him. Giving her an intense desire to kill him now. The mouse then ran for his life as the cat was close behind straight on its tail. Narrowly escaping the mouse dived into its little hole in the wall where the cat couldn't fit.

The cat reached her paw inside but the mouse was just out of her reach. The cat then sat there and stared back at the mouse waiting for him to come out. The mouse however, did not move a muscle and the cat neither did move. Both sitting there and staring back at one another.

The mouse then looked around inside of the hole. He began biting at the wood and began digging. Soon, he made his way elsewhere in the house away from the cat who continued to stare as he got away.

Although the cat had murderous intent for the mouse. The mouse did enjoy seeing the cat go about her day. Especially when she slept, how at peace she was. The mouse knew the cat was alone in the big house. So, the mouse waited until the cat was asleep and it went and laid his head next to the cat.

After a while the mouse felt movement and it opened its eyes to see the claws of the cat strike it just before it died. The cat then slept a peaceful night knowing that she finally rid herself of that wretched mouse.

The next day the cat was strolling her way through the halls. Making her way to her favorite window to look outside but she heard a noise. She turned her head and there he was, the mouse following right behind her. The cat ran for the mouse again, catching him and killing him. This time for sure. Checking the mouse again, the cat knew with his mangled body, for sure this time he had died.

The cat then went and lay on the windowsill and enjoyed the ritual sunrise of the morning. Later that same day, however, the cat saw the mouse peeking around the corner. She chased him down, killing him again. This time, however, she watched him to see what would happen next. *Just how was this rodent coming back,* she thought.

Hours passed but still no sign of life from the mouse. He was surely dead, yet still the cat stared at it intensely waiting for some response. Just then, the mouse twitched. The cat jumped back in response.

The cat even though she was shocked, stood its ground and watched the mouse as he put himself back together. His wounds were closing and his bones were mending; he was being completely healed.

The cat was in shock at what she was witnessing. As the mouse found that he was right in front of the cat once again, the mouse went and scurried away from the cat. The cat was left there with only the memory of what she had witnessed, thoughts completely blank at what she had just seen.

The cat then for the rest of the day went into the night, spied on the mouse and hid from it. She started noticing several things from the mouse as she followed it. The shadows that lingered past the mouse, stayed in each room. *How peculiar,* she thought.

Avoiding the shadows, she continued her stalking. Soon she found the mouse trying to avoid the shadows that were following him as well. Once the mouse had stepped into one room to escape one shadow, another one would be right on his tail.

The cat enjoyed watching the mouse in peril, feeding her own sick pleasure, the mouse ran for his life trying to get away from whatever those shadows were.

Finally, though the mouse came near the cat, that lured the shadows towards her as well. The shadow started attacking the cat but she leapt away from it before it could hurt her. The mouse, however, could not escape it this time and was killed by it.

The shadow soon disappeared after leaving the mouse in a mangled state once again. The cat then took to a shelf on the far end of the room and watched from afar. The mouse had recovered, good as new. Then the shadows appeared once again to torment the mouse.

The only problem was that the cat was a target too. Soon, the shadows spotted her as well. So, the cat waited until the shadows had inevitably got to him. Once they were done, the cat picked up the mouse and threw it outside. The cat now every time she saw the mouse, would kill it and throw it outside. And if the rodent was seen inside, the cat made sure to give no mercy to it. Sightings of the mouse soon became less and less, and eventually the cat finally could rest easy.

4

_____

As me and the boy continued through, images began to form and eventually we're in a house. I looked back but all I saw were stairs heading down. My mind wondered as to how we ended up here but I gave up trying to reason with any of it.

I then heard some footsteps coming up the stairs. The little boy holding my hand starts shaking again. Tears started coming from his eyes as I tried to calm him down. I turned around and saw that it was a girl, one who looked to be about my age.

"Hey, get away from that thing!" she yelled at me.

She grabbed the nearest thing she could find which was a bat and pushed me out of the way. Swinging hard with the bat, she hit the little boy hard, breaking his neck.

As he fell over, she continued to beat him with the bat. His head was crushed and his body was mangled. With each swing of the bat to his body, I heard the loud cracking sound of what could only be his skull breaking. Blood shot up from his mouth, like a small geyser. He then stared up at the ceiling and struggled to breathe with his mouth full of blood and with a little twitch every few seconds, he stopped moving.

The girl made sure that he was dead before turning back to me. She looked at me, eyeing me up and down, sizing me up like she wanted to fight me.

"Are you okay?" she said.

"Why did you do that?" I snapped back.

I surprised myself by how angry I was by this. It's not like it was my first time seeing a child get killed. Add that to the fact that I hardly knew him at all.

"Trust me, just stay away from that. The less you know about it the better." she said. "Hey, do you have a place to live?" she asked.

I looked outside a window nearest me and saw that this place is completely different from where my mom and dad were.

"Well, I sort of got lost." I said.

"Yeah." she responded. "Well you can stay 'round here if you like." she continued putting the bat down. "I mean, my mom and dad haven't been back in a while now so, you know. Just been me, myself, and I."

"How long have they been gone lately?" I questioned.

"Two years." she said casually.

"Two years?!" I repeated in shock. "Did they say when they were coming back?"

"No, in fact I just woke up one morning and realized that they were both gone."

"Don't you get sad and lonely without seeing them?" I asked her.

"No, not really. But I do get bored sometimes and I do have a ton of freedom to do whatever I want now, so it evens out." she said. "By the way, I'm Katlyn, and what's your name?" she asked while extending her hand.

Only then did I notice some of the blood splatter on her shirt, as well as her arms, extending all the way to her hands. I began to raise my hand to shake hers but seeing the blood of that boy on this girl that just took him away, I just couldn't bring myself to shake her hand.

She looked down as my arms lowered down. "I get it." she said. "I mean, look at me. Very inconsiderate of me to do so, right?"

She seemed to have come to the conclusion on her own that it was uncomfortable for me to touch her with blood on her. She would only be half right, not with just anybody's blood; it was the boy's blood on her. She killed him and that for some reason, now that deeply saddened me a lot more than before.

"Hey take a seat on the couch." she said as she pointed towards the guest room. "There's a lot of movies you can watch. You can keep yourself busy with that while I wash up."

She went into a room and closed the door behind her. I stood there for a second and reluctantly went towards the guest room. I pried my mind away from the image that I saw. Why was I getting so worked up over a random death?

This feeling suddenly grew inside of me and it began to make my eyes water. This feeling was the same as when I saw MITH get into trouble. I tried to shake the thoughts and feelings away, but the thoughts just wouldn't go. I felt the drops wash down my face and I sat there staring at the pile of movies, one of the cowboys caught my eye.

Something touched my shoulder and I jumped. I turned in shock to see that it's Katlyn who looked worried. A smile crossed her face, after that she guided me into the kitchen.

"Hey, have a seat." she said again. I did as she said and she sat across from me at a wooden table. "Um, I didn't get your name when we met." she said nervously with a smile as if it were awkward to bring it up a second time

"Oh well, I actually don't have a name." I said as I smiled back at her. Her face lit up with amazement.

"Oh, your smile." she said, "It's so beautiful." I kept smiling but not at her, just past her. The little boy, poking his head out from the guest room, stared back with great cautiousness.

"Are you alright?" she said. She looked over to see what I was staring at. The boy hid in the room as soon as she turned her head.

"I'm fine." I said as I grabbed her hand for reassurance. She looked at me with concern like I had gone crazy but disregarded it, at least it seemed.

"Well, I know what I should call you. your name is Smiley." she said with great delight. "Hey, let's go and watch a movie and see some cool stuff."

I followed her yet I was worried that she would see the boy, but upon entering the room he wasn't there. I wondered now if I really must be going crazy but then I felt something tug at my leg as I made my way to the couch, I looked down and it was the boy. Katlyn turned around and wondered what caught my attention. The boy however ran off into another room before she could spot him. She did spot the small bloody handprints on my legs where he grabbed it.

"Where did he go?" Katlyn asked me.

"I don't know." I said looking down and pretending to be shocked, but I was not very good at pretending and so Katlyn didn't buy it.

"What are you doing?" she said. "Listen, Smiley, that thing is very dangerous. Now you need to tell me where he is." Her tone had grown more assertive, but I stood my ground, telling her that I didn't know, but she still doesn't buy it.

"Why are you doing this?" she said as she rushed past me into the other room. I grabbed her arm, stopping her in place.

"Katlyn, I can't let you hurt him." I said as my tone grew more assertive as well.

Her face twisted in confusion. "Why not?" she said.

"I honestly, don't know why I feel this way but I feel like this is something to do with someone I know. It's a familiar feeling I get when he's around." I said. "Like he's connected to me, it's weird."

"That's what I mean when I say he's bad to be around. He does that to lure you in so he can hurt you." she said as she tried to continue into the room but I stopped her again by pulling her arm.

"What are you talking about?" I said to her.

"He comes around and something bad happens every time. Whether I stop breathing or start getting a heart attack from out of nowhere. He gives me a death stare and watches me die. It only happens when he's around."

"I can't let you hurt him again." I said to her.

"No, Smiley, We have to hurry before something bad happens again. We have to get rid of him."

"Don't worry about the boy. That's just fuck meat going around now."

A big man suddenly appeared before us and he was giving us a sadistic smile. In his hand he was holding the boy and he was crushing him. I could hear the bones slowly cracking.

I ran to him and bit his leg, in retaliation he kicked me off and stomped on my face. I felt my nose running blood then I was unable to get up from how dizzy I was.

He grabbed Katlyn and his face lit up.

"Hey, I remember you." he said. "You're that woman that butchered me. Tell me how this feels." He bent one of her fingers backwards and Katlyn screamed in agony. "Hurts like a bitch, doesn't it?"

He then bent another one of her fingers backwards and tears ran down her face. I tried to get up but he just kicked me back down again. I tried to speak but my words only sound slurred and incomprehensive.

He kicked me in the stomach again and I almost blacked out. I could tell that he was holding back or else I would have been crushed by him when he stomped me.

He then slapped Katlyn and smiled as he lifted her up. "Why are you like a little kid now? Oh, Zefron is going to love you guys."

Just then a plate was smashed at the back of his head and another man towered over him, it was my father. He got one of the shards from the broken plate and stabbed the man in the eye.

"C'mon, Teresa. This way." a voice screamed in the back. They pulled me into another room and I was followed by Katlyn. The man that had attacked us ran, but just before he could enter the room, the door was slammed right in his face.

I jumped to my feet, expecting him to come bursting through the wall but nothing happened. That's when I looked around and the scenery was totally different. We were in a totally different location from before.

I fell down right on my hands and knees and I started coughing up blood. In the background, I heard Katlyn breathing unevenly from her two broken fingers. I gazed around before I tried to stand. My mother ran towards me and helped me up. My father then guided Katlyn to a couch on the other side of the room.

I held my stomach and felt it convulse, I vomited several times before I was able to make it to the other side of the room where Katlyn was. I looked up at mom and tried to speak, but the pain was so great that it froze me every time I opened my mouth. I began to hurl again, and the color began to change to bright red.

I breathed heavily trying to regain myself and taking my mind off the pain. My dizziness was getting worse as I tried to stand. Lying back on the couch, I held my head trying to focus, then three knocks could be heard. It came from behind the same door that that man had attacked us.

No one would open the door at first but then a soft voice called out. "Hello."

My father rushed towards the door and opened it, it was his mother. He hugged her at the sight of her relieved to see her; he took one step back.

"Ronnie. please, forgive me. He wanted it this way. It was the only way to bring you all together." she said.

"What are you talking about?" he said.

"He wants us to work for it, Ronnie. His own sick twisted little game." she said.

As her eyes turned watery red, a hand came over her shoulder, grabbed my father by the throat and tossed him back into the other room; he then pushed the old woman inside the room I was in and closed the door behind him.

Along with the rest of us in the room, we were trapped inside with this mad man. My mother then got to her feet after making sure I was well seated on the couch.

"Oh looky at the tough lady here, standing up for her kids. Bitch trying to protect her little angels. Let me show you how pitiful a shit like you can really get, yeah."

"Damien." she said as her eyes grew wider.

As the man came forward, the old lady held on to a foot trying to hold him as best she could. The man kicked her with his free foot. While he was distracted, my mother lunged forward to him but the man smacked her down with ease. He then put his foot on her head so she couldn't move anywhere, pinning her down to the floor.

He then grabbed the old woman by the throat and put her against the wall. He then slapped her, "What trying to do? Double team on me, huh?" he said.

She struggled to get free of his grip, but she was too weak. He laughed at her effort and slapped her again.

"What a fucking scared fuck, you are." he said slapping her harder. "You of all people tried to fucking stop me." He says while slapping her repeatedly each one harder than the last.

Soon she whimpered, with her eyes now making streams that rolled down her cheeks.

"Oh, is that how they cried while they were in the basement? While you sat there watching what he did to them? Or was it when you were upstairs eating in his room? How you could hear them screaming in pain, hoping somebody would save them." he said, taunting her.

"Why don't you stop crying you fucking cunt?!" he continued, looking irritated.

She stopped making any kind of noise. Soon her arms went limp and fell to her sides. Still he continued slapping her and now with every slap, blood splashed across the floor from her face.

She was breathing heavily, now as soon as he let go of her, she dropped to the floor like a sandbag; face first. I couldn't see her face but judging from the blood that came flooding to the floor, I didn't think I wanted to know.

My mother who was on the floor, still struggling stared in shock at the old woman. The mad man then stomped my mother's hand, breaking it. A sound didn't escape my mother's mouth but her face showed the pain.

"Damien, no." she said to him.

Damien was the mad man's name, I thought. My mom was in trouble but I couldn't move no matter how hard I tried.

He grabbed Mom by the hair and threw her into the wall face first. She was bleeding by the nose and struggled to get her balance as she tried to get to her feet. He picked her up and slammed her back down to the ground. Blood came pouring from her mouth as soon after she hit the ground.

"Don't come and rescue me." she said.

He stared into her eyes and said, "You, along with that man and this woman deserve something worse than hell itself. It's a fucking joke that you came and actually tried to do anything right. When we're no better off when you try to do things right."

He slammed her face down to the floor and began to pull her hair. Mom tried to stop him but she might as well not even try because of how much she was in a daze.

He then snatched a good portion of her hair out. My mother began groaning in pain as she felt the bloodied spot where her hair used to be.

Still holding on to what's left of her hair, Damien dragged her by it, coming towards me and Katlyn. Still holding her hair, he stood in front of us.

"Now, repeat after me." he told her. "I'm sorry that this bitch couldn't save you."

My mother didn't respond back, but I knew she could hear him perfectly fine.

Hearing no response from her, Damien grabbed me by the shirt. "Say it!" he repeated back to her in a threatening tone.

"I'm sorry that this bitch couldn't save you." she uttered back to us.

He then turned back, threw her to the ground and kept stomping. Mother tried to fight back but she was completely overwhelmed by him. The beating became more horrid that I began to look at Katlyn. She was struggling to get up, she was halfway to passing out. Something is choking her, however it's letting her get just enough oxygen to stay conscious before taking it away. she couldn't even move if she tried.

I tried to move but my body couldn't do it. I tried to scream but my words came out mumbled.

Soon I did hear screaming but it wasn't my own voice, but from someone else's; my father.

He came in, but like my mother and the old lady he was struck down. He stumbled towards the doorway and struggled to stand using the door.

Damien then came forward meeting him in the doorway and was about to grab him when he screamed in pain.

The old lady was biting his leg just above his heel. Tearing his flesh from his bone as she did. This provided my father with enough time to slam the door. This caused Damien's head to be crushed in between the side of the doorway and the door itself. Dad continued to do this until he eventually collapsed to the ground in a daze.

My father was about to do it one final time when my mother called out for him to stop. My mother couldn't even stand, had to crawl her way to him. Father saw her and helped her up.

"It's Damien." she said to him, trying to grab my father's arms but was too weak to get a grip. My mother, who was too weak to stand, sat down with her back against the wall. Her eyes seemed distant before she closed them.

Father's eyes had now widened, and it seemed as though he had seen a ghost. "Of course," he said. "In the picture you were so clear to see, but now it was hard to tell. Holman and his games."

"Damien." my father said, looking at him.

Damien then rose to his feet and rushed my father to the wall.

"I'm sorry, Damien. I'm so sorry." my father said to him. He stared into his eyes and kept staring until he realized Damien wasn't breathing, why he wasn't even moving.

"He's lost to you." a voice cried out. Just then everything froze.

An old man walked into the room and stared at the scenery before him. "You have no relationship with him and he doesn't know who you are besides what his mom says about you. Why, I'd say I know him better than you ever did."

He walked to the old lady and stroked her hair. "You did good, princess. I'll let you sit out in your room for a while. When we're done here, there will be a special little girl." he said.

"She's a troublesome one. I find it difficult to be friends with her but you could bring her around." he continued before returning to my father.

My father's face grew red. "Get the fuck out of my head." he said.

"I'm not trying to get into your head, boy. I have no desire nor need to do so. You are doing all this to yourself." the man said.

"I saw him as the man he came to be." the old man said, as he rubbed Damien's neck. Father then tackled the old man and threw him down to the ground pinning him down with his neck. The old man laid emotionless there for just a moment.

He formed a smile across his face and got to his feet with his neck stuck sideways before returning it to its upright position.

"Do you want to know how he died? That little girl killed him. That little girl named Katlyn killed Damien right after your son got through getting his rocks off."

Father then punched him in the face but the old man laughed at him still. "After all that time you were beating your wife, you think you could swing better than that."

Father then lunged for him but the old man smiled. My father phased right through him, the old man was still standing there as if he had never moved.

"Try again. I'm not convinced that you really mean it. I might as well keep playing with your family again and I'll have them tell you what I did to them one by one. Maybe that might motivate you enough." the old man said, teasing my father.

Father tackled him and grabbed his head slamming it to the floor. Grabbing anything his hands touched, lamps, chairs, desks he used to smash his face into the floor until they broke apart as he was using them. Then the old man responded once he was done, "Do try harder if you can, please."

Father's face turned bright red and tears started streaming from his eyes; he grabbed the cord attached to the lamp and started strangling him with it. He looked into his eyes as he did it and grew even angrier at the sight of him and pulled harder on the cord. He dared not look away. Father was absorbed in this moment.

Harder and harder he pulled with the cord now digging into the old man's flesh. Father watched as the old man's eyes turned red with tears pouring out. His neck was being crushed, now shrinking from the sheer force father was applying to him.

But then father's eyes rolled back as he grabbed his chest in pain. I could see his veins pulse in his face as he fell to the floor unconscious and sweating profusely. I looked at my right now and Katlyn seemed unconscious as well however still breathing.

The old man then turned, smiling until he saw me and the smile on his face disappeared, his eyes were locked firmly on mine and he was frozen still like a statue.

I felt a sudden weight come off me and I could move freely now. That same similar feeling came over me again but now it's so strong, I ran to him. My eyes began to burn as I finally recognized him and I embraced him tight.

There was no care for what he had just done; all I cared for now was just this moment.

I saw him as I've always had, my little boy. He placed his hand on the back of my head slowly and hesitantly it seemed. As his hand touched the back of my head, I knew his other name, Holman and everything along with it.

Other names began to surface, along with their history.

Something else eventually came to mind, he didn't let me see it. He knew it was better for me not to and it's something that had been happening to him this whole time. Since the beginning all the way to this moment right, something that would stay with him.

The brutality that I've witnessed until now couldn't hold a candle to what he's been doing to himself. Terror began to fill my body. He's feeding off it right now, not only this madness that just occurred, but to what was happening to him right now. Something that was getting worse with me standing here. It's beyond what I could possibly imagine.

I tried to back away but he tightened his grip, I stepped back with more force but he pulled me back. *I can't stay here*, I thought. I shoved him back.

He finally spoke. "A bit carried away for a time, can't seem to stop." He stared at me and as I shook at the sight of him.

I could see him grow more rapidly and his breathing. He was taking deeper breaths that made his shoulders rise and fall. He stepped closer and for every step he took, I took another step forward, I noticed this and stopped myself.

He got on one knee and extended his hands for me to come.

"I can't." I said to him, looking at what he'd done, I just can't. "Why?" I began to question, "Why."

Holman responded, "I want to see everyone burn along with me." He pauses for a bit. "To watch it reach the breaking point then the build up from it. Before they're thrown deeper into the rabbit hole, only to be torn apart again. It's all too beautiful to me."

"It's fun to play with toys, even more with myself and better when you put up a story. A story needs puppets and I'm one of them." he continued

"I want you to be right alongside me for all of this."

"I don't want this." I said. "None of this."

"I'm sorry. I'm deeply sorry for this but I won't stop. You wouldn't care less as long as I'm here." he said. "I'll hold off for a time and you'll call for me and then you'll understand what I mean."

Closing Pages

Everything turned white and as Holman disappeared in the color, he knew he failed once again, He started out with the annihilation of everyone but had gotten so absorbed in whatever this was and lost his way proving once again how much of a fuck boy he was. He cared not however, now he'll get to hear them squeal and he would be right there among them.

Sitting at the dinner table, my family came in to surprise me on my eighth birthday. I jumped up at the surprise and saw a big magnificent cake coming in, being carried by my mother and grandmother. The sight was magnificent.

My father told me to blow out the candles and I did with my brother joining in, too. I got my slice and took the first bite out of the cake, it was delicious!

He sat down in the cold darkness, remembering nothing but her warm smile. Soon he would have that again. She would always come for him and she would do it again. Now, he just had to wait, she would tell him when.

Oh that lovely smile, he started changing at the thought of it now. His face stretched and turned black. With red indentions in his face to resemble a Smiley face that you see on those advertisements.

Mr. Smiley sat down in the cold darkness, he saw a being standing before him. The being multiplied into several others of himself filling his vision. The beating never stopped and the brutality will never stop.

Mr. Smiley was in an open dark space. He saw that he had no appendages and that he was blind and deaf, except for the fact that he had a higher sense. He knew what was going on. This however gave an even greater sensation of what he saw and heard what was going on. Along with that, he was able to picture it perfectly in his mind exactly how it played out around him, like watching a movie really. The being appeared before him and with one flick of his finger, destroyed Mr. Smiley's body.

The being then found that he was growing exponentially stronger. Mr. Smiley's pain spiked to even greater heights.

The being then punched Mr. Smiley; as the punch was thrown, he created infinite timelines and new dimensions, when he threw another, he destroyed them all. The being felt his strength growing even more.

Mr. Smiley then formed back; feeling the being grow stronger. The being dashed toward Mr. Smiley; he was moving faster than an instant and he hit Mr. Smiley again. The space around them was changing everything, infinite on all levels and beyond that was going crazy, just by the being's movements.

Everything on all levels of existence and matter itself. Everywhere that there was to be and not to be was constantly being destroyed and created again. With just the slightest movement of his pinky. Mr. Smiley knew one thing that would remain untouched however and he made sure that she would be untouched.

There was no concept of time for it was destroyed. There was no place or setting, new laws of physics and science were being created and destroyed. Everything was constantly changing in how they were operating. The omniverse and all that lay beyond it was no more, for now it was something else entirely different.

Mr. Smiley knew this.

Mr. Smiley then put everything into its normal setting as if it never happened then created a new space that was white. This space was stronger than the one they were originally in, so it could withstand more of this being's power. The being however laid a beatdown so savage that eventually he destroyed the space, so Mr. Smiley created a much stronger space.

After a while the being destroyed that as well, and so Mr. Smiley simply went on his way to repeat this. The being then multiplied and continued to beatdown Mr. Smiley who was no longer being destroyed but still felt the pain of all the hits he was given. The being kept multiplying, eventually shooting a blue energy beam at Mr. Smiley and other copies of him did the same. More kept doing the beatdown, while others joined in keeping the beam on him; zapping him.

The numbers kept stacking and would not stop. Mr. Smiley eventually had to duplicate himself to have more hands on him, this would go on and on.

Absolute, No Limit, he thought as he started to make things even more absurd.

This would by choice be what occupied Mr. Smiley's time for now, among other things.

Epilogue

Her whole family lay around the room, with the exception of her grandmother. Her mother painted on the wall, her brother hanging from the ceiling fan by his entrails and her father exhaling, taking his last breath on the floor. As the last breath escaped from her father's mouth, the last page had been turned.

The boy sits with Amy on the couch in silence.

The boy looked at his Amy and imitated, as if he's turning invisible pages.

"Yes, of course." Amy said smiling. "I'm ready for the next story."

www.ingramcontent.com/pod-product-compliance
Lightning Source LLC
Chambersburg PA
CBHW030207130726
47898CB00012B/917